Penguin Books
Casualties of Peace

Edna O'Brien was born in the West of Ireland
and now lives in London with her two sons.
She has written *The Country Girls, Girl with Green
Eyes, Girls in their Married Bliss, August is a
Wicked Month, Casualties of Peace, The Love Object*
(short stories), *A Pagan Place* and *Zee & Co.* (all
available in Penguins). Her latest book is *Mother
Ireland* (1976).

Edna O'Brien

Casualties of Peace

Penguin Books

Penguin Books Ltd, Harmondsworth,
Middlesex, England
Penguin Books, 625 Madison Avenue,
New York, New York 10022, U.S.A.
Penguin Books Australia Ltd, Ringwood,
Victoria, Australia
Penguin Books Canada Ltd, 2801 John Street,
Markham, Ontario, Canada L3R 1B4
Penguin Books (N.Z.) Ltd, 182–190 Wairau Road,
Auckland 10, New Zealand

First published by Jonathan Cape 1966
Published in Penguin Books 1968
Reprinted 1971, 1975, 1977
Copyright © Edna O'Brien, 1966
All rights reserved

Made and printed in Great Britain by
Cox & Wyman Ltd
London, Reading and Fakenham
Set in Monotype Baskerville

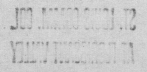

For Rita Tushingham whose coat it is

It was late at night, all the houses were in darkness and all the people in all the houses fast asleep. Willa came hurrying along a road that was not the one she inhabited but that led there. Three short roads led into her own road that was roughly divided into three sections, upper, middle and lower. She lived in the middle section not far from the railway bridge. A large brick house with a double gate, white woodwork, a dormer window at the very top, the front paved throughout with uneven slabs of concrete and consequently no place to plant flowers, but two tubs filled with clay had been put there to serve as flower beds. They were at either end of a wooden railing that guarded the drop from ground level to basement level. The flowers in these tubs varied with seasons but at that time there were red geraniums in bloom and a white mossy flower that propagated itself most agreeably, even got in the cracks between the paving stones. The geraniums would have lost their colour at night, they would simply be tall soft blurs, but Willa could see them, boldly red, in her mind's eye and see the hedge newly clipped and recall her disappointment, because she liked a hedge to be thick and shrubby. But he cut it ruthlessly, Tom did. Just as she reached the end of the short road that led into her own road she let out a cry. And no wonder. She found herself without a key. She tried both pockets, delved into her handbag but knew, even as she tried, that the key was indoors on the side

7

table where she'd put it earlier that afternoon, having taken it from her handbag, when she went out to inveigle Tom not to clip the hedge down to its twigs. She could have put a mat, or a stone, to the door, but she didn't. She brought her latchkey in her hand and later put it on the hall table under a display of roses. It would be there still.

She entered her own street and was on the edge of the kerb about to cross the road when the noise of a car reached her. She saw it, coming at a lunatic speed from the lower end of the road and luckily she did not try to beat it because she would most certainly have lost. It stopped as it got to her, stopped with a weird facility. There were two men in it. One of them wound the window down. They had come flush with the side of the kerb and as they did she backed her right foot but did not follow it up with the left for fear of betraying herself. She stood quite cool, quite brazen. The second man turned off the ignition. She recognized them not by their faces but by their intention; which was to kill her. The one who spoke looked at her, around the belly region. Indignant, she gave her head a little toss, of defiance. The spill of her hair moved with it. He smiled, the merest leak of pleasure on his indecent face. The horror he would do to her. Up to that moment her killer had always come alone. He had been one man who arrived at any hour provided it was an unexpected hour, he surprised her in the doorway when she stopped to lay milk bottles there, or in the hall-way at an hour between daylight and dusk, his hand coming between the banisters of the stairs as she mounted to go to her bed. Now there were two. One of the men – it did not matter which one – spoke. He said:

'Is there a theatre around here?'

'Yes, you go left and left and then right.' The untruth

was quick, fluent and convincing to all but two men who had come to kill her. They fell in with the ruse, they pretended to believe, and they drove off thanking her for her help. She ran in the pathway of a neighbour's house. This house had no doorbell and no knocker, there was simply a dull, chrome letter-box of a contemporary type. She raised the heavy flap and let it spring back, making a fiendish noise. When there was not a reply at once, she lost hope of there ever being a reply at all, and resolved to cross the road anyhow and hide, perhaps in the porch or in the miserable hedge. She took great confident strides. In crossing the hour changed from night to day and the darkness gave way to light. But far from this being a solution, it brought to her notice a worse monstrosity. Her own house had its number changed. Or, almost her own house. She knew it though some of its features were cunningly altered. The two halves of beer barrel were gone, for instance, therefore the geraniums; the paintwork was dark and peeling, but it was her house because she knew its position exactly. It was numbered 104, and the house next to it was number seven, and the house beyond that number 33. (The correct numbers for these houses were 37, 39 and 41 respectively.) All order had gone from the street. And there was a different type of numbering. Flashy gold lettering posted on each gate. Whereas in real life the numbers were in black over the fanlight and difficult to make out. Bright gold, brazen untruths. Each house was a little altered, but not so altered that she could not recognize each one. The stained glass above her own door was undeniably hers. One house that had glistening Snowcem walls was smothered in ivy, and a garden that possessed two magnolias gave growth to another tree altogether, a little stunted tree with no chance of blossom, tar patches smeared on to hide the scars where it had

9

been lopped. She was not alone either. There were the sounds of schoolchildren from a back garden, the back garden where they played each day and often upset the drift of her thoughts, and farther up in the end section of the road there were two men with empty coal sacks slung over their shoulders as they emerged from a house. She could hear the children singing, 'Found a peanut, found a peanut, found a peanut in a bin,' and she could get the smell that coal lorries always dispensed and that she'd once ascertained to be a mixture of fish oil and coal; she saw the men too, their faces smeared with coal, one shoulder each, drooped from the habit of putting the heavy sacks on that particular side. She heard, then caught sight of it as it turned back into the road, the green Ford motor, and she knew that they were coming to get her. Absurd though it was, her lie to them gave greater justification to their deed. She could not walk, nor run. Her bones had turned to water. She gathered her coat around her and put her hands, her jellied hands, into the pockets for shelter. It was daylight and there were witnesses, but none of these factors helped. Her death was not their responsibility. They were children with terrors of their own and workmen with woes of their own. No help at all. The green car stopped right at the spot where she was standing and the men got out at either side, losing no time at all.

*

Willa McCord wakened, backing into the rungs of her brass bed. In a dream she had just been slit in multiple places. At once she began to fight herself out of sleep. A most difficult endeavour. Her eyes were open but she was still in sleep, her body that is. It was as if her body and her limbs were sunk in a deep vault of sleep and coming out of it entailed journeys through passages of lesser and lesser sleep. She tried with all her might, forcing her legs, her hands, the very extremities of her body to waken up. Sometimes the terror of being sucked back into the vault threatened, and it was both a terror and a solution, but gripped by resolution she fought and struggled until at last she was awake and possessed of her faculties. There was dribble on one corner of her mouth and she occupied about one-sixth of the space of the double bed, so bunched up was she. She looked; fearful, expecting to find someone, or something, in the bed beside her, or below her. But there was nothing there, there was the empty space of the double bed, the lower part of the sheets unruffled, the green necklace like a rosary hanging from one of the brass posts where she'd put it when she undressed the night before.

'It's all right, it's all right, it's all right,' she said, now fully awake. She wiped the dribble first with her wrist and then, face down, wiped it on the pillow-slip, and said:

There is no panic, I am not a child, I am not with Herod, I am not afraid. I am not a child, I am not imprisoned, I am not afraid, I am not dead, I am not dying, I am not being followed, I am not in the wrong, I am not afraid.

She said the words quickly, unthinkingly as if they were a prayer or a set of multiplication tables. As indeed they had become. Old words often said. She reached through the brass rungs of the bed-end and lifted the curtain to see the hour. Daylight. Dawn-red ridges in the sky. She almost wept with relief. A sun too red on the tip of the earth, above it the patches indiscriminately coloured like bloodshed in a child's painting, and farther up channels of pink in lighter and lighter hue so that the last pink verge faded imperceptibly into the vast tissue paper of white sky. She looked at that rising sun in the sane sky as if she was looking at it for the first time in her life – or the last. The tube train went by and the necklace on the bed-post rattled, its rattle outlasting the noise of the tube by several seconds. Normal life. She thanked God, and then began to upbraid herself for such an illogical dream. Where was Patsy, where was Tom? And where the spare key they kept under a stone for just such an emergency? Where were all the steady things and why couldn't she run? Why did her body desert her so? Why had she let doom take charge of her? She lay back and stretched to try and unwind the coil of pain in her stomach. Only that she knew it to be unlikely she would have sworn there was frost. She brought the covers right up to her chin. Frost in October. Anything possible. Once in the month of May snow came on a Sunday night and met her when she was journeying across a field with her mother who was troubled about something. She tried very hard to think of the snow without getting it involved with any human recollection. To think of light snowfall, sometimes blowing sideways, and appearing to come not from the sky but from an earthly region, sometimes falling in single discernible crystals, and sometimes in showers falling senselessly upon the world. Hard and therefore hail; soft and therefore blossom, blossom or snow matted along a black branch that grew down, falling snow, falling feathers, falling breadcrumbs, falling blossom, or whatever it was, falling freely and thickly and benevolently on a free, empty, abstract, horizonless world. Like manna. She managed to quiet her thoughts and gradually the knot loosened, and with the covers tight around she soon felt warm.

At eight the footsteps went down the stairs, she heard them not by the actual thud of each step but by the creak of the wood. It was an oak staircase she had specially put in, and defying her own superstitions she had asked for the banister ribs to be spaced well apart. Then he crossed the hall and she knew that she would hear no more because he opened the door gently and closed it from the outside just as gently: drawing it until the latch grazed the lintel, then putting the latchkey in and turning it and holding it until the latch reached the socket hole, then releasing the key to allow the latch to slip quietly into its appointed place. Thief-like. She smiled at his consideration of her, the dearness, the constancy of it. More than a year now, and he had never gone down the stairs hurriedly, and he had never slammed the door. If she was asleep he never wakened her, if she was awake his progress never jarred upon her nerves.

Not even a breakfast. Had it in a café along the way – two eggs, four rashers of bacon, a loaf of bread, fried. In the evening he told Patsy how much it cost, and said that in future he wanted his breakfast cooked at home, but never got it.

'Dear, dear Tom.' She smiled again at his consideration of her. Since Tom and Patsy came, her life had a new order, a solid peace. She felt happy as she thought of the day ahead: it was going to be sunny, she and Patsy would drink a little wine at lunch, find some reason for celebration. Forget about work, the past, the present, the whole foolish ramification of real or dreaded woe. The thought of this happy day unfurled before her and, like when a concertina is opened out and a little music escapes from the bellow, a little of the happiness already felt was languishing within her.

*

His wife Patsy listened with the same fervour but for another reason altogether. Then she jumped up. It was easy to grab her things – what use would he have for frocks and lady's shoes and corsets? It was the stuff they both owned that was the bugger. Wedding photos, vases. The coffee set! Lovely cups not too small, with a blue flower on the white china. Beautiful tall pot, similar but smaller jug. Split it? That wouldn't be right. Neither one thing nor the other. Pity they'd ever been given it. She wouldn't be in a stew now about who owned it. Goods are a torment. She began to wrap the cups in newspaper, then stopped. Better pack other things first and then survey the space situation. She stood before the mantelpiece where the photo confronted her. They were so young. Two eejits! She looked a fright. Had a home-perm the day before, done by one of the girls. First night he was on for it all the time, wakening her up. How little she knew! Nothing. We don't know anything when we start out. When did it go wrong? Never went right. What made her suffer him at all was the way he used to walk her home from dances and buy milk for her from one of the machines. She said it was a nursing home she worked in, didn't mention that it was for incurables in case he might get nervy. Never laid a finger on her except dancing, when tried through jacket pocket. But they all did that. Small things that she hadn't noticed when they were out, she noticed soon as they shared one room. The noise when he swallowed, his smelly feet! Tell me when you're coming! Didn't give her a chance! Racing away two minutes after he went in. Is it big enough for you? First few months all right, bearable. No sign of anything doing. Lads on the job joking him. There must be something wrong with you he'd say. Why her? Still he must have felt it. Lads on the job had christenings and things. That was why he grew so pass-remarkable. Nice bit of stuff he'd say of a television hostess, someone who wouldn't be seen dead with him. He felt it. Rough in ways then all apologies. Shone her shoes for Sundays and the time in bed with pleurisy bought her four chocolate cakes. Loved to cut a dash himself – new shoes, flannel trousers, a blazer with brass buttons. A kid! But kids had to be with other kids. After twenty-five a man had to stop shitting around. No use asking what's for tea, it didn't matter what's for tea. You weren't going to be happy anyhow. Begrudging him everything, even your thoughts, shutting him out, smiling to yourself about something and he asking what and not telling by silence or by 'mind your own business'. Minute to minute torture that's what it was, and meanness and bitterness. Diabolical. At times he begged. Home from work begging and grimed, the way no man should ever have to be. Then the moods. Then he gave up sulking and cried. Loved getting told off. Hereditary most likely. Father spent his life in bed having horse liniment rubbed in him for eczema. No feeling for anyone else. When the darkie got killed on the job didn't bat an eyelid, didn't go to see the darkie's widow or anything like that. Made a joke about it. Part of his nature missing. Not because it was a darkie either. None of that type of shit. Looking at the telly every night. Timing her if she went out of the house for a bag of chips. The number of pullovers she knit. And five hand-done rugs. It wasn't natural at all. Willa not putting the rugs on the floor saying she preferred furry ones. They were like animals all over the house, white fur rugs, looked like they were breathing. Willa took off her shoes and stood barefoot on them, Willa was not normal. Maybe the two of them would have a bit when she was gone. On rugs. Jungle stuff. It was cruel leaving without warning but this was no time for softheartedness. Could bear it until the other fellow came on the scene but from then on it was fierce. Couldn't but compare them. At first it made everything easier. Happiness. The thought of him in her wherever she went. The glory of it. A bloom on her skin, it certainly had some benefits attached, better than the facials Willa had. Usedn't to flare up either when Tom raved away about being the youngest man in the army and the President coming to see him and congratulating him on his valour. Valour! Making tea, and spying on the fellow that was doing a line with a sheep. In Kildare it was, in Ireland, flat country populated with sheep. All that raving about getting priority going in to the pictures and doing manoeuvres. Came from having no father. Terrible risks attached to being a child. Ignored his dirty habits too, like peeing on the coal shed. If Willa knew! The way she found out at all was getting coal late one night and seeing it shiny. Said there must be a cat because no end of mice could pee that amount. Tom started to laugh, like a child, and she sang dumb and let Willa think it was a cat. No use being too honest. A mug's game. Lads at work had part of the Kinsey report, loose sheets torn from someone's copy. He brought them home. Said 'there's a few moves here we might follow.' Ashamed to look him in the eye, in case he saw her secret. She and Ron could knock spots out of any Kinsey report. After that the awful dream of him in the bath and his yoke falling off and he yelling for her to help and she trying to get it back on and not being able because her hands were slippy with the water and she saying 'sit still, sit still you bastard' and he yelling and crying. Guilt most likely. Daft dreams are. Reached out just to make sure he was all there and him stirring and thinking it was something else and getting on her. Was it big enough? He knew bloody well it wasn't a question of size. But none of that mattered once she had the other fellow. Looked upon it as her duty and did knitting in her head or made out lists for the shops. Guilt too, giving in about the car. Like a child the night he brought it home, driving it up and down the road. She had to sit in it. Willa had to sit in. Whistling he was and singing different lines of songs to the same air and then he and her went for a drive when all the traffic was died down and he said 'It's what I always wanted.' Glad for him, that he had a wish come true. Next day he got her the ring. Sinful waste. A bit on the small side. The comrade of it in the window in the High Street. Four pound ten. Sudden display of emotion made her tear into a shop and get him a cover for the steering wheel. Red velveteen. Put it over his head like a hoop. Tears in his eyes he was so grateful. Played Irish tunes on the back of soup spoons. Strutted around. Shouldn't have got him a present, letting him think all was well. She'd leave the ring. He could pawn it. She washed her hands to ease it off and dropped it in the soap dish. The stone had quite a sparkle when wetted. A four-pound-ten sparkle at least! She left business things on the mantelshelf where he could easily find them – the television licence and the car insurance. He'd faint but he'd get over it. She put his cuff-links there too in case he'd be going anywhere special, like to see a solicitor. They were a present from Willa. Dull silver, classy. She often borrowed them. She wouldn't borrow them any more. Often they both wanted them for the same outing but he always gave in. Poor Tom. Funny how a small thing like that hurts. 'That's a thrush' he'd say if they heard a bird. 'Blackbird' she'd say. 'I mean a blackbird' he'd say. Knew damn all about nature but that wasn't the point. Had no opinion of his own. Would fall in with anyone's views. 'I'll cut the dog's tail' he said to a woman down the road. Woman thought he was off his noddle. Daft things he said, 'Let's tour the South' or 'I think I'll go to Paris for the week-end.' Great with kids though. Got on well with kids, played 'I spy' and tricks with pennies in Coca-Cola. No good with people, that's why they never went out. Made a right fool of himself the first night they met Ron. Playing darts. Tom raving away. 'There are fifty ways of killing a man by using only one blow.' Demonstrated on a pencil. Broke it in half. She bent down and picked one half from the sawdust floor and Ron bent too and got the other half. Their faces close to the sawdust looked at each other. Their foreheads nearly met. In that position he asked what brand of cigarettes she liked and then he walked across and got her a large packet of her favourites. Tom said it was time to go, after only one drink. Ron said good night as she went out. Could have ended there but there was some demon in her. Went back to the pub a few nights later, asked his name, told some rigmarole about how he had a bet with her husband as to who'd win the general election. He never came in week nights, but was a regular on Fridays. Friday she was to be found sitting inside the door, all cool and lackadaisical, togged out with clean clothes; combined knickers and corset affair that cost the earth, summer dress buttoned down the front, sandals. He wasn't surprised. 'How's your husband?' 'Fine, he's got night work.' 'What are you having?' 'Rum and coke.' 'That's a funny concoction.' 'I'm a funny concoction.' That started it. Under the table while the drinks were coming. A new dress. Half the bloody buttons came off. Don't sew them on firm in factories. A date for the following Friday. For all Fridays. She went prepared. Drinks first with some of his mates. One night she couldn't wait. She was bursting, so was he. They took one look at each other. Fuck his mates. They'd be back, he ordered two pints and gin and orange for the lady. The pub full of noise and argument, people sniggering as they went out. Up close to him, his serge suit warm and rough. Up an alley in Peckham Rye. Beautiful beautiful Peckham Rye. You was that happy you didn't think there was ever going to be a next day, or a next minute. Policeman sneaking up with a 'Do you realize what you're doing?' Not half. Name and address demanded. Gave his own. Brave thing to do with a wife and kids. Didn't stammer either. Trepidation for weeks. Nothing came of it. Having to go in after and dry in the ladies' with a wad of toilet paper, then a splash of French perfume from the machine and out for gin and orange and fresh urges. Getting home and having to tell a pack of lies. One lie never enough. Four months of it. Well it was all over. Things never turn out the way you think. Pictured it going on for years, the lies, the thrills, pub garden on summer evenings like Zanzibar, days in between as long as months, washing, ironing, going to bed early, all unbearable except for the letters to him. Lads on the job thought it was from the pools. Then the bit about being thrown out of the flat. Off to Liverpool. More housing. Clean air. Missed Ireland. Was a groom there for several years but left to get married. Shotgun stuff. Five months gone. Married in Lent. Three kids since. Wife and kids sent to Shropshire to cousins for the time being. Dumped. Another on the way for sure even though he didn't say so. Ethical!

'You might as well come,' was what he said.

'Is that the way to ask a woman?' Discussed ways and means by which he could entice. All shameful. Face of his got as red as his hair. Bad at speech. Only time he wasn't shy was when he was in surging away and having bites. No stammer then. Had a stammer sometimes at unexpected moments like on a bus or buying a drink. But never when he came. So they had to face it. Agreed that they would have to part, but ended up deciding they couldn't. Liverpool to be Zanzibar. He'd go first, get a job on the docks, get a room, a bed, and what more did they want! They'd face the music when they were together. A golden plan. He'd go one Friday, she'd go the next. They were sitting side by side on a park bench.

'Will kiss you now,' he said, and did, then pushed her down and habit being habit pulled her dress up and got it in, and for a full five or ten minutes they ran the risk of public prosecution. She was not prepared. 'What would we do if anything happened?' he said. 'Do you think it would have red hair?' she said to tease him. He was ashamed of red hair and wanted to apply boot polish to it. She saw him off at the station and gave him a small bottle of whiskey for drinking on the train. Said he wished she could go with him. She wished it too but had a few accounts to settle up. She hated journeys; looking out at the scenery, what was there – chimneys, football pitches filled up with water, fields, animals? Still with a few gins and a load of shitty magazines she'd get through, have a sleep maybe, because they'd be awake half the night. She half-packed, then stopped and began the letters. She was nervous as hell. A sure sign when she began one thing before finishing another. The letters were the worst part.

Dear Tom, I am going away for good. I have thought about it and we are not for each other. It's not that I hate you or anything, it's that I don't love you and living the way we do is dishonest. There isn't anyone else. Don't take it too badly. It will be all over next year.   PATSY

Dear Willa, I am going away. I have wrote to my sister and she thinks it's best, I have wrote to my mother too but haven't heard. Tom doesn't know but he will now. He will give you all the help he can until you get someone. He is good at doing the garden and pulling the grass up between the stones or anything like that. I want to do something for you to repay you but it will have to be later. Well Willa, I hope you can read all this, and try to forgive me. I will never improve now.

     PATSY

She sealed them because if she kept reading them she would be tempted to change words and changing words was lunacy. She left the coffee set. To hell with it. It might only get broken being carted from one place to another. Might be out of place too in his den. She had one letter. Sent to someone called Josephine O'Dea. 'Who's Josephine O'Dea?' Willa said. 'God knows!' Willa was told. Wonderful the powers of contrivance. Called her darling. Could have called her anything because no one knew. She tore the address off in case he met the wrong train. Although she was going and knew she was going and had nearly packed she couldn't see herself getting out at Liverpool and being met by him. She could see it up to that point but it was too glorious to envisage beyond that! She closed the case and with her foot she pushed it under the bed; then she went down the stairs, humming, like it was any other morning in her life.

At nine o'clock, the set hour, Patsy brought the tea tray. She placed it on the bedside table and walked across to draw the curtains, a function which she performed with a clamour. To be sure and waken Willa. Once she had caused an embarrassment by finding Willa still in sleep, but with the covers thrown back. Ever since she entered with a rumpus and made various noises before drawing the curtains and admitting daylight.

'It's time,' she said brusquely. Her back to the bed.

'Is it?' Willa said, knowing well what hour it was. Patsy stood, as was her habit, looked out at the garden and commented on the day.

'It's warm,' she said. Willa sat up and looked too, down the garden to the one beyond. Two stretches of pampered lawn. A low wall in between. The lawns were in shadow because of wide trees, in shadow and covered with dew, the sounds of the city came from somewhere beyond, but agreeably as if noises had been selected, filtered and carefully delivered. A calm life. An edifying view. Gas chimneys well out of sight. Lawns pearled. 'Yes I am a lucky girl,' she thought, and reached for a cardigan to put over her shoulders.

'I had a nightmare,' she said, her voice silly with self-pity.

'The sauce was too rich, I knew it,' Patsy said and, turning, looked upon her mistress – pale face, big grey

22

eyes, long blonde hair a bit greasy, a youngish woman but a wreck. Pale and wrung. All ready for the business of suffering!

'What the hell is wrong with you, you're like a scarecrow,' Patsy said. Her sympathy was in her gruffness.

'Nothing,' Willa said. Once comfort was forthcoming there was no need to press the agony. Patsy inquired into the nightmare. Was overjoyed to hear that it concerned wrong numbers on gates. She shrugged and said there were worse things in the world and Willa said that was certainly so.

'We might whitewash the wall today,' Patsy said. The wall dividing the two idyllic stretches of garden was grey and at times Willa complained of its greyness. 'Might do you good to get fresh air,' she said, but thought 'Might make it easier for me to make a hasty retreat when I need to.' Willa wasn't going to the studio for a bit. She had worked too hard on a window and the concentration got her down. Supposed to be clouds in a window. More like clots.

'We'll begin it anyhow,' Willa said.

'We'll begin it and end it,' Patsy said. One thing she never spared was her energy.

'How do you know it was the sauce?' Willa asked, a slight grin on her face. Patsy's opinion she valued. Patsy, the mother without child, the worker, the worrier, Tom and Willa to care for, a house to help clean, grocery lists to make out, paper serviettes to buy for the morning meal and linen ones to iron for the evening meal; Patsy with a hundred schemes of her own. Inventive too. Like putting the pheasant plumage in a pitcher, their ends stuck in a boiled potato to keep them from toppling over. Patsy simplying life, frying bacon, playing cards, cracking egg-shells with a flourish, endowed with a child's directness – 'Why do dogs pee so often when they're out?'

'Because *I* had a nightmare,' she said in a flat voice.

'The horse mushrooms?' Willa said, softly. Patsy moved a step towards the bed, her face giving in to sentiment. Willa remembered everything. Over the years they'd told each other many things and when Willa said 'the horse mushrooms', Patsy was less alone in her world. She bit her lower lip, and frowned. A thing she did to fight off intimacy. No day for it.

'Your Ma . . .' Willa said, but in a suitably mannered way. Night after night in bed with Tom, drowned in the foul air of his smelling feet, Patsy dreamed of her mother, and was transported back to the big houses where her mother worked, mainly for bachelors. Willa knew it all, getting it in bits and pieces over the years. Willa had never seen photographs of Patsy's mother but took it that they were alike in physical appearance: round robust women, blue eyes, jolly faces, frizzy hair, arms like the boughs of trees. Patsy's mother brought home souvenirs from the big houses, cigar boxes, calendars, peeled pearls that had been discarded by visiting ladies, stiffeners from shirts, corset spires. For what? To put in drawers. 'I'm remembered in their wills,' she would say. No wonder. To find her own mother against a wall, as Patsy did, her own mother with her skirt up around her middle, and the long thin rake of a bachelor bent so as to get it in and her mother saying, 'Wait Sir, wait, till I get the ashes cleaned out,' and Patsy in sly-soled shoes creeping in on them. 'What do you want?' her mother asking. 'Nothing,' Patsy said and vanished. A thing like that was hereditary. That night she slept in the corner of a cornfield and took an old trench coat off a scarecrow to put round her. She knew there would be search parties out. She could hear their voices coming over the fields, calling, calling her name, training the beams of their lanterns into dark corners, putting sticks down into dark badger burrows, calling, finding her, carrying her home, her mother's arms around her saying 'There, there, there,' apple fritters and custard for the reunion. Devil a bit of it. She fell asleep waiting for them to come. When she wakened it was morning and there was a horse breathing over her. Such a fright as she got. The horse's breath warm, like a person's breath; terrifying. Little mushrooms had come out overnight. She tried to get the horse interested in the mushrooms.

'Nice, nice mushrooms,' she said in a coaxy voice. But the horse kept breathing and sniffing. She raised her arm to shoo him away. He made dangerous swoops with his neck, swoops and mad jerks as if he was going to lose his reason and trample on her. His hind legs in a state of pounding. Finally she risked all and began to crawl out under him. The black under-belly of that horse enveloped her as she crawled inch by inch watching his shanks, in case. The journey under that hanging belly was as long as she remembered anything as being. When she got home her school lunch was on the table beside her satchel. Bread and sugar. Same as always. That night her mother cut off her ringlets. Said the weather was getting warmer, said there were nits in her hair. But nits got in short hair too. Her mother held it up, the long rib of hair with the nit clinging to it, clinging for dear life, recited the life history of a nit – 'For nine days it clings to the hair, then turns into a louse and begins to case the head, and immediately lay more nits.' The supply was wizard. The thought of it made your skin creepy, and you itched and itched until you tore your scalp and never knew whether the speck of blood on your thumbnail was your own blood or that of a louse. All this Willa had got out of her. In one way Willa knew her better than Tom did, or Ron, or any other living person.

'No, the other shitty one where I cut the carrots wrong,' Patsy said defiantly. She sat on the end of the bed and watched Willa's lips parted by the thin rim of the china cup.

'Poor Patsy,' Willa said. Poor Patsy. To each his own predicament. Patsy the server. On her first job at fourteen she cut the carrots roundwise instead of lengthwise. A disgrace to the British nation. A slander on the doctor's wife whom she worked for, got the sack, after she'd done the wash up. She wrote to the Queen of England and enclosed a stamped addressed envelope, she said, 'I can't go home, I thought you might be interested in a scullery woman.' Short and sweet. After seven days she took up work in a home for incurables.

It was heaven. Thanked no matter what little errand she did. A friendly atmosphere. Incurable people falling in love and pawing each other under plaid rugs. The hundred little decoys that kept their hearts up like what kind of soup for Sunday. All tinned soups identical flavoured but still they liked to know what kind. Willa asked to hear the same stories over and over again. Like a child. 'What did you say to the Queen?' Willa asked.

'You know well what I said.'

'Tell me again,' Willa said and stretched until her toes touched Patsy's thigh. The covers between them of course. Patsy thought it was no day to look back, but a day for looking forward.

'We'll use brushes, rollers are no good, they don't get into the corners, what do you want for dinner, I mean lunch, there's a bit of pheasant left, that sauce was too rich, wonder if he had a nightmare,' and laughed in herself. Couldn't tell Willa the one about his yoke falling off, because of no man in her life, except that Herod maniac, and coffee-coloured creep with the bracelet and his name on it. Auro no less! The cheek of it. And he not white. Couldn't tell Willa the facts of life. Could talk about dreams or the carrots lengthwise but not about doing it upside down. Funny, and Willa thought to be a woman of the world.

'Poor Tom, he didn't have a cup of tea,' Willa said, her toes pressing against Patsy's thigh, and circling – the way the webbed feet of hens looped round their perches at night.

'Poor creature, it's a meat breakfast he ought to have had,' Patsy said. 'Sleeping it out, over-oiled the alarm clock so that it wouldn't go off, did it on purpose, I had to shake him to get up, looked at the clock after he went, swimming it was, got all over the bedspread . . .'

Patsy raving away seemed to take no notice of Willa's toes or of Willa's face lit by a little unseemly flush. Her first known memory with a girl. Her cousin Pauline. Coming home from school they climbed a wall and went into a wood to gather primroses for a home-made altar, then Pauline linked her and they dropped the flowers somewhere and vanished into the depths of the wood, saying nothing. Pauline put her standing against a tree, lifted up her box-pleated gymfrock, left her knickers alone and slid her hand up under the leg, saying nothing, her hand making its way until it got to the hair. The pleasure was sweet and trickly, even sweet to remember, but the hair there was raw and hard. Had it just started to grow? She put her own hand there too, to either prevent, or encourage the proceedings. Or both. Otherwise how would she have known what it felt like? As secret as the tabernacle. The flap of loose skin where it all was – the pleasure and the pain, the pain and the pleasure. Not that she looked. They were safe in the

wood. Pauline always asked for booty – silk handkerchiefs or a shilling. Willa always agreed. Afterwards she
felt ashamed and ran to the top of a hill. The sky was
there, the sky and plenty of cloud milling around. The
wood was dark, dizzy, a prison of a world, with no way
out. But nice. Back again. Then or later. Nice going in,
thinking of it, nice, nicer than golden syrup, a bit like
that. Didn't take long. She could not remember doing the
same thing in return. She did not touch her friend there,
too cowardly, like putting your fingers into the unknown, into a mystery. Even then she was passive. Even
then she was mean-hearted. Her fingers, twenty-four
years later, did not retain any memory as to whether her
friend felt raw and bristly or had locks that could be
wound round and round. Her eyes of course would not,
because they never looked. They couldn't. She looked up
at branches, or down at the leaf-mould, and never let on
to Pauline what was happening, though Pauline knew by
the look on her face when the agony broke. They had to
be careful not to be found by any of the workmen from
the sawmill. Especially by one nicknamed 'the cuckoo'
who prowled the wood pretending to look for trees that
were in danger of falling, but really looking for girls.
Pulled his pants down, said 'Watch me do pooley,' said
it to more than one girl. The story was awful, it did not
bear telling, it did not bear listening to, it never pro-
gressed beyond that first detail of the man drawing his
pants down. It was calamitous, worse than cancer, worse
than encountering the mad women along the road,
worse than the thought of people dying in hospital.
But the worst thing of all was what she and Pauline did.
Maybe Patsy did the same, or had it done to her. Maybe
Patsy crept in too, to the madness of the woods and felt
the hair that was raw and unseemly like the first days of a
beard, and risked everything.

'Patsy,' she asked harmlessly, 'what have you got against beards?'

'Jesus,' Patsy said rising. 'At this hour of the morning, and the breakfast not ready.'

The wireless was on and the grill was on downstairs. Sometimes the house smelt like chapel but in the mornings it had the nice smell of grilled bacon.

'Get up,' Patsy said. Willa thought Patsy must be lonely. A mistaken conclusion, in fact it was nerves.

*

Willa picked up the pile of letters; the first was from a television rentals to say they'd been under-charging her for several months, precisely from the day when she had a second aerial put in, in order that they could see programmes on a highbrow channel. But none of them used it. She threw the letter from her. Some day she would be poor again and lists of her extravagances would present themselves in order to torment her. The second letter was from a male admirer to make it known that his interest in her work was acute. (Willa worked in glass: figures, windows, birds, crucifixes, mermaids, numerals, saints and martyrs all made of glass with glass expressions to denote emotion.) Should she reply by saying 'Thank you, but I would like you to appreciate the fact that glass is cold and chilling to the touch. Glass is not human. Neither is the glue with which I bind it. Nor the acid with which I treat it. Glass breaks, glass is fragile, it does not endure. You can look at it, you can look through it, but you do not discover anything more the closer you look, glass is monstrous to sleep with. Handling and holding glass you yearn for flesh.' Certainly not. He would be around by priority motor car and she be then revealed for the fraud she was. Rich and rare were the gems she wore. In other words she was a virgin. Though tampered with.

She didn't open the others. She read the postmarks quickly. He lived in Hampstead. Auro, golden boy. For a while she expected a letter, now she read the postmarks but no longer expected the letter.

For a time she thought he would be back. He had a habit of appearing and disappearing. His job made it possible. She knew him to be weak, inscrutable and sly, but with a tender heart, unlike Herod. In the end she let go. It took weeks to get him out of her mind. Silliest things stuck: like the time when they swapped shirts because she admired his and he had no objection to wearing hers. Silly thing that she'd taken over seriously. Still she learnt: to be more cold-hearted, vigilant, glacial. She was not angry with herself. New joys like the antibiotics invented fresh and freak diseases. The love for him and then the pain was nothing like the Herod experience: the love had more good nature and the pain though less dreadful was merely ageing. He'd come into her life like many another to purchase one of her glass works. Mostly she worked on windows, for churches, schools, and the odd factory, sometimes she did a bird or a figure and these were bought privately. He telephoned first and four days later he came to the studio. He had the palest Negro skin she had ever seen. Skin with a touch of blue in it. Roads newly tarred came to her mind, the tar not dry, the colour neither blue nor black but something in between. Nice to get that colour in glass. Delicate featured except for his nose which was flat. Calf's eyes. Lids mauve, the eyes behind them instead of being trusting as befitted their size were shrewd, canny and alert. A constant smile as if life was a good joke.

'Who smashed your nose in?' she said.

'I did,' he said. 'A man can't be perfect, it gets people's backs up.'

And here she smelt a resemblance. Once she had said 'Why are you called Herod?' and was told 'I'm not, I am Herman, I have renamed myself in order to please my enemies.' No rile in the voice. The rile kept secret.

She should not have asked about his flat nose, it was a mistake. She rarely talked to any of her customers, she rarely talked at all, between her and the world she had built sheet upon sheet of coloured glass so that when she looked out or they looked in the gestures were all distorted and the voices barely heard. Some thought they knew her but they were deceived. Like a dog trying to catch a fly with a window in between, their endeavours were wasteful. No one would ever catch her again.

'Do you think it will be of great benefit to us when animals talk?' she said.

'God forbid it,' he said.

'We won't be so bored,' she said.

'What makes you think they'll be any better than people?' he said.

'They'll take longer to be worse,' she said and they smiled at one another. He looked around. The myriad and tormented world of her figures. A plain glass window with a white blind, not drawn.

'That's a fine window,' he said.

'It was put in by a mason,' she said, 'who has no teeth, but when he gets teeth he's going to eat a steak.'

He opened his mouth to show his which were extremely white and somewhat forbidding. He bit on nothing. She offered him an apple. In his mouth the juice of that apple extracted totally, the flesh ground to a pulp, because he chewed so. He said it was a good apple, crisp. He tended an orchard once. She asked in

31

what country. He said 'This country.' He was second generation.

'Orchards must be nice,' she said.

'If you're a wasp – yes,' he said.

'I'm sorry,' she said, 'I was showing off.'

'You're all right,' he said. And she wished she had something to show him or something to say that would be above and beyond the dross, that would leave a nice taste in his memory. She stood before him and what she said was, 'Keep me the little apples for jelly, they're sweeter.'

But he was an orchard man no longer. He worked on films as a cameraman. She moved away disappointed, with herself. What had he in mind? What exactly did he want? A pyramid, he said, for the living-room.

'Beryl likes the things you do.' He did not explain Beryl, he did not have to, Willa grasped it. What kind, what colour, what height, what price, what design. They discussed it but in discussing he told her other things. There was no reason for him to tell her, he just did.

'Beryl would like this studio, Beryl likes French cigarettes, and the cinema better than the theatre, French cinemas most. We have the place done all in white, except for the bedroom which is Victorian, flowered wallpaper, lace curtains, lace bedcover and so forth . . .'

A man silly with love.

He jumped off the bench, then wiped his hands of dust and began to walk. In love with Beryl but not opposed to a little frolic on the side. She saw him in toga, the bedcover really, carelessly gathered round his body.

'I would rather one in black lace,' she said.

'That's because you haven't seen the white,' he said. The word white came starkly across the room, through glass, through silence, through the drawing board behind which she had hidden, the word fraught with a beauty it had never had before. Veils. Gauze. Hollyhock. The moment when boiling sugar begins to thread and each thread before it darkens, the white of morning and the white of moonlight. Did they ever in their urgency fling themselves on that lace coverlet and profane it with their hot love?

'Just like a piece of cake, her hair knotted behind her, not looking whacked or anything,' he said, and Willa tried not to hear. She asked God to spare her their intimacy.

'The midwife not come and only me and her. "Get ready to deliver," she said. I put my hands over her mouth, cupped, pretended it was oxygen, in no time she breathing it, earnest, there was I blowing into one end and she breathing it at the other end, believing in it, I had to keep going . . .'

Greater love no man hath, than to deliver his own child. A third-generation black baby, known in the dictionary as a quadroon.

'I suppose one can be made to believe anything,' she said tartly.

'Am I boring you?' he said. He must have divined her unease.

'Why should it bore me?' she said. 'I was just thinking how in mythology, anything could become anything else, a woman finding a bedraggled cuckoo took it in, fed it at the breast and it turned into a man and slew her.'

'I can top that,' he said. 'A man kept a tiny baby alive all night by letting it suck on his nipple, until its mother arrived . . .'

'Yours is a nicer story,' she said. Men and babies, it was all the same. They needed the mother to come weighed down with milk. But where were mothers? In shops, at shoe sales, in the hairdresser's, in waiting-rooms, on couches, the milk going sour in their emancipated glands.

'I need a mother – man, woman and child all need mothering.' She wished she had not said it because it turned out that he had never suckled, never known the woman who bore him She left him soon after he was born with that name on a tab round his neck, that name that was to defy and be in direct contradiction to the pigment of his skin.

'Then you are a woman-hater,' she said. Men either were or were not but at first you could not discern because of little tricks of behaviour.

He came across the room, how quickly or how slowly there was no telling, and as only happens in dreams, in madness, and among strangers, he put his arm round her, first one, then both and he clasped her and said through the spill of her hair, 'You're nervous and bitter, you shouldn't be either nervous or bitter.' Held by him. Every particle of thought gone out of her as if the blood stopped flowing to her brain. Conscious of nothing only those arms, covered by blue shirt. She did not – she dare not – speculate on what would happen next. He could not see her face since he was behind her. Her nipple under the spatula of his roaming thumb did not sing for joy. He put the other hand around her ribs and gasped at her thinness. She was leaning against him, the dark furze of her being atremble. Her desire was her trembling. She must not encourage him. She must testify to another involvement, a great love. By declining him she knew that it was not that he had to go without – there was Beryl – but that in some mysterious way she would drain him of a little of his well-being. She freed herself.

'There is no need for us to be cheap,' she said, her

back to him; in the corners of her eyes tears. She said she must open the window. He said open the window. The difference in his manner noticeable. The sudden softness of evening. Tenderness. Skin the colour of dusk. She thought of offering him a drink, another apple, or her lips. No lipstick either as tell-tale on his handkerchief. She offered nothing. Across the room her voice cracked with nervousness and the unaccustomedness of the situation said, 'So you have children.' Three he said. One by Beryl, two by someone else.

'That's plenty,' she said.

'That's what I think,' he said, in a sensible voice. The remark delivered to himself, he raised his lids but did not look at her. His mind on other things. She watched: he jutted his lower lip out and completely obscured his top lip, a habit when he was thinking of something. Because of course they met again, and again. They invented excuses. Crude, patent but workable excuses. She would make a taller pyramid, a better one, she would cut the glass at another angle altogether, tell another story in the way she arranged the small violet cubes; speak secretly through it to him. These tricks sufficed. He talked less of Beryl. She could see her influence on this waning passion and was shocked by her own felony. But greeted him in an honourable voice. He came at odd hours, he would say 'Maybe Tuesday,' but Tuesday would pass and no sign of him. Strategy was out of the question. He had two wives. He'd been an orphan, he'd had two mothers, and no mother, he needed two wives and no wife. She understood.

'Come as you wish,' she said. How many hours had she knelt on the hall floor, her eyes level with the letter box listening for his motor car to come thundering down the road. Hours of pointless sacrifice. She would have hated to be found at the window waiting. Even her waiting she hid from him. Solitary love, solitary passion, her desires gone underground like the streams and rivers in the limestone country around part of Ireland and part of Yugoslavia.

No apology when he did come. The way he handled it, exemplary. 'How are you?' she said. 'Still black,' he said, or to Patsy, 'Have you got the butter out of the fridge?' as if the too-hard butter had been presented to him a moment, rather than a week before. It was impossible to be peevish, or to say 'Where have you been?' because he didn't accept reins. He liked to be free. Broke down her strictures so that she said 'Come when you want.' Thawed her a little, at first they sat side by side but then he commended her to sit on his knee, and she did.

'I'm too heavy,' she said.

'Stop worrying,' he said. She pretended to be at ease for a little while then made a second attempt to stand up. He held her.

'Do you ever relax?' he said.

'Do you ever relax?' she said.

'Often,' he said. 'But when I'm relaxing my teeth are clenched.' They laughed. Why did he see her? He loved Beryl. He said true. Why did he see her then? She knew why. She was new, so was her weight, so was her nervousness, he wanted to pass through and decompose her. If only she'd stop shaking. He felt for the calf of her leg, gripped it firmly, then stroked it softly. Told her how he was master at stroking cats. He waited on them to come home at night, then waited until they wanted it, then stroked them the way they wanted.

'You're still worrying,' he said.

'I'm heavy,' she said.

'You're not heavy, say "I'm not heavy".'

She made two attempts then rushed it. His arms came

36

round, reassuring, comforting, and he hummed some foolish little tune.

'How long since you were happy?'

'Never,' she said. The preposterousness of it.

'I was happy the day I met you,' she said then, but timorously in case there was some sort of obligation on her remark.

'That's good, that's very good,' he said, feeling her toes as if he were feeling for broken bones, then he bent down and smelt the flesh, but when his tongue sought out the crevices between those toes she explained nervously that they had collected clay from the garden, and soon she tightened, closed, and recoiled from him.

'You have to . . .' he said, 'I want to give, give, give, I want you to come for a month at a time until your eyes are gone back in her head from coming, come, come, come to me.'

'Can't, can't, can't,' she said, in one way and another. No way of telling. He would have to be her to know. He would have to have lived through all the attempts; lying in bed feeling the bones at the side, and along the top, then trying to dwell with her mind and risk with her hand, and finally learning to weave her fear into a glass-bound ocean or a crown of thorns. He tried with words, moods, hands, mouth, persuasion. Moments of near surrender, then terror again, her saying, 'Can't, can't, can't.' His wanting her more. It was like that, him wanting her, her wanting him to, but only in her head, her body unable. It was like the need to run but finding the legs buried in slime.

'The oldest living twenty-six-year-old virgin,' she said. It was his duty he said, like going to war or putting out a forest fire, he would deflower her beautifully. The flower they would keep for ever as if the relic of a saint. She would see. Gently does it. His hand roamed to where her skirt ended. A skirt with a frill, the frill ribboning out, a life of its own. His hand beneath the frill.

'Can't, can't, can't,' she said. Weren't there plenty of other women in the world whose voluptuousness she could never compete with? He ached for her. In the corners of his eyes tears.

'We have to,' he said. 'Bed is bed. It's not kissing, not cuddling, not anything else, bed is bed.' This disheartened her more. She said she would think about it, she would prepare.

'You were not happy the day you met me . . . you were eager.'

'And am I eager now?'

'You are eager and you are petrified.'

'One or other will have to lose out.'

'Make sure it's the right one.' He rose to go.

'I'll ring you,' he said, 'even though you never answer it.'

'I'll answer you,' she said.

'Look, three rings, then stop, then ring again, and it will be me.' He wrote on a pad and tore the sheet out. From his jacket pocket he took a clothes peg and fixed the sheet to the telephone flex. Like a white handkerchief waving in the air, for all to see. He meant it when he wrote it down, he meant it when they walked up the road in search of a taxi, their separatedness reaching out to one another, their hands not clasped, their sadness confirmed in their laughter (tears were for the next day); and they had to pass of all things a hedge of wild yellow roses with skimpy petals but a drunkening smell. The heartbreak of that walk got confused in her mind with the smell and it accompanied her for days, for weeks, whenever she passed the hedge in fact. The cargo of memory inherent in that smell of yellow roses. Not so much the memory of what they had as what they might have had. And what cuts deeper than regret founded on nothing. He meant it when he wrote it down but next day he must have given it serious thought and metalled his heart. The flower on the sheet too vivid an image to create, the burden of her too much. She waited. She worked. Her grief realized in her saints and in her sinners. A pearl-grey window commissioned for a concert supposed to be a soothing sky-scape with clouds moving about, no clouds those but ovaries floating in a sea of trouble. At the end of each day she cried, tears did not come to the rescue of her eyes, she cried with her body, hands out, his love the alms they asked of life.

'How dare he,' Patsy said and took the note down and put the clothes peg in a bag along with the others. Same kind of peg.

'I didn't like it,' Patsy said, 'the way he ate your steak after clearing his own.'

Worst of all when the telephone rang and she let it ring three times then expected it to go silent before ringing again, which of course it didn't. The letters saved her. They were at once her consolation and her nourishment, through the letters she pleaded her cause and though never posted they absorbed the juice of sorrow. Delirium, strange outpourings and the drunkening smell of yellow roses.

The kitchen was bisected by sun and in one side – the dim side – dust on the rise through the air and Patsy mixing whitewash with water. The wireless was on. A light male voice delivered an item of news:

A dentist suspecting that his wife had left him went to the wastepaper basket of his local post office, found the draft of a telegram she had dispatched to a male friend, followed his wife to the airport and murdered her. Shortly afterwards he gave himself up, in the Natural History Museum in South Kensington, London.

Heard by Tom, on the job, told to him by one of the lads, yelled to him because of the vibrations of the pneumatic drill. Tom said she deserved it. They laughed.

Heard by Auro in his Victorian bedroom as he sat picking the threads of the lace coverlet. Beryl wouldn't talk. He was home late the night before. 'Beryl talk.' The most innocent thing in God's world. Met a girl in a dance dress walking along the street. The dress was two lengths of white gauze stuff sewn together along the top, the sides open. Her thighs in white stockings for all to see. She was crying. She had nowhere to go. She had crashed a party. She had heard that the Aga Khan was going to be there. They told her he was dead. She said his son then. They said his son was abroad. They gave her a drink, in the hall. Guests came to look at her but soon lost interest, and she had to leave. Nowhere to go she told

Auro. Made the dress herself, for the occasion. The news of the party had been leaked to her by a junior in the hairdresser's. The head hairdresser was booked by the hostess for the whole afternoon. Nowhere to go. He bought her a coffee. She dried her eyes. She smiled. She said that when she got rich she would have pink sheets and hundreds of pairs of shoes. She would keep her jewellery in banks all over the world. He brought her home. He made the mistake of telling Beryl. Sad little, tatty girl with spurious hopes. An 'Airfix' Cinderella. But Beryl couldn't see reason to distinguish. Beryl the interrogator – 'Where were your hands, where were hers, why did you talk to her in the first place, if I'm on the street does any man come to my rescue.' He shook his head. Women's voraciousness. He tried to explain how pathetic it was but she turned away. He wanted her. For both their sakes. He put his arms around her but she rebuffed him. Made him think of Willa; on the south side, chipping away at her glass, a waste of a woman, too awkward to love, full of nonsensical hurt; but with echo. 'Beryl fit it on.' A coat to winter in. Just the thing for Canada and the snow, being as she insisted on coming with him. Got for next to nothing on the set. 'Give it to one of your pick-ups,' Beryl said. 'Beryl listen.' Beryl turned up the radio and rejoiced when she heard the story of the passionate murder.

Heard by Willa in her own cool kitchen after lunch, as she took a last draw on the cigarette before assigning it to the ashtray. She tried to pity the murderer, she couldn't. She went on staring at the cigarette butt:

A frond of dead-grey ash, the glow underneath smouldering away, the manufacturer's name in thin gold letters at the very bottom of the cigarette paper where it would never be smoked beyond, this with a view to immortality, the fawn tip with uneven citron-coloured specks, the sponge-like underneath. She remembered other hours like this, with Herod, when she knew the features of a teaspoon off by heart. But she could not pity the errant man.

Heard louder, clearer and more menacingly by Patsy than by any of them. 'Jesus,' she said into the bucket. She had been stirring slowly, one hand stirring, one hand on the rim of the bucket to keep it from flying all over the floor but when she heard the news she began to stir fiendishly with both hands. They might have her traced. Willa would think it was nervous breakdown or some shit. An s o s on the wireless – 'Woman in dark coat weighing eleven stone thought to be suffering from loss of memory . . .'

'There's madness in love,' Willa said gravely and rose.

They proceeded as they had planned to whitewash the wall.

*

Patsy walked jauntily. The bucket bumped against her hip, the paint inside agitating to get out couldn't reach the rim. She would apply herself to this for a couple of hours, then make tea, leave the tray on the lawn and go. Soon to be over. One thing she'd miss the garden. And Willa. Willa bettering her over the years, saying 'Listen to this', or 'Don't say I done, say I did'; called her into a room once to show her a single-string pearl necklace forming the figure eight on a bureau, the sun coming in and every pearl purple and pink besides being pearl as well. They had battles over letting the sun fade the furniture. Willa won. She'd miss all that.

'Come on, we wasted enough time,' she said. Willa with her face stuck in a rose. She lifted it out. Pollen spotted her nose. Sometimes, like that, she looked lovely, a smile like a child, her hair very white in the sun and straight like a ship's sail. Terrible life, alone always, hidden ways. What did Ron call them. Fetishes. And where did he pick up that dirty information. He would have to account for his actions.

'Here, forty-five bobs' worth of camel hair,' she handed Willa one of the new brushes. Urging Green Shield stamps on her in the hardware shop. 'Stamps my arse,' she said, 'you're winning anyhow.' She accepted bribes from no one. She told Willa. Willa laughed. She wanted to go away with Willa laughing. She dipped the wide brush into the bucket, tapped it against the side to shake off the excess paint. Did it slowly as a demonstration. Just because they were out of doors there was no need for Willa to waste paint or to splash it all over the place. Willa was to behave exactly as if they were in the sitting-room and the rugs were in danger.

'But I can enjoy it?' Willa said, falling in with Patsy's bossy mood.

They began.

There can be something hypnotic about painting a wall. Partly due to sun and partly to its own thirst the wall ate and drank every drop, every molecule of paint. It was marvellous to see. The way the wall drank in the paint and became ready for more. There was only an instant when a patch showed very white, because in the very act of beholding it the excess white was being sucked into the body of the wall to merge with the plaster grey. It was not industry that induced Willa to work so rapidly but her longing to re-create that startling whiteness.

Patsy was breathing quickly. By contrast the brushes had such a soft, lulling sound. Nervous breathing and the slow strokes of the camel brush. Like the two sounds birds made with wings. One flappy and busy before they took off for the day's pilgrimage, one restful when they came home at night and accommodated themselves to boughs and branches. With the same set of wings. If she were a swallow she would soar very high to the loneliest emptiest part of the sky, away from the irritation of fellow birds, nests, eggs, repetitiveness. Away with the clouds. Coming down for food and a little spring wooing. As the semen darted in her she would fly, letting it spill out in a wild jet of betrayal. No aftermath. Freedom, freedom, freedom. Even as a bird she clung to female-dom. No doubt as a bird her songs would be dirges.

'I love steady noises, lawn mowers, motor engines, clocks that chime,' she said in case Patsy hungered for a word. Once she looked in Patsy's writing-pad and saw written to a sister, 'Willa is good to us, but she is whim-sicle.' To forage through Patsy's letters was another way of escaping into Patsy's world. To live a little of her bleak life through Patsy. To find comfort there.

'There was a case in the paper of a woman coming back from Amsterdam with a diamond up her arse. They got it,' Patsy said, pursuing her own thoughts. How thorough the bastards could be.

'I know a man that likes his shoulder tapped while he's making love, just tapped and tapped,' Willa said performing the same function to the wall. Auro told her that about himself in one of his many attempts to deflower her. 'He thinks it's from the time in the womb when he heard his mother's heart beat.'

'Oh womb scutter,' Patsy said, impatiently. She was in a right state. The diamond, the maniac dentist, the man in the paint shop saying 'I see you go up Peckham way,' all got her on edge. Now, womb stuff. Any minute pregnancy.

'You'll be paid for this separately,' Willa said. Patsy must be feeling exploited.

'Oh Christ it's not money,' Patsy said. The last thing

she wanted was Willa thinking that money had split them.

'It's just that . . . well, I wasn't going to tell you,' she said, and even as she began she regretted the impulse bitterly.

'Me and Tom have had it . . .'

Willa thought it was with her they'd had it. She made fluent and noble promises. She would have a second entrance made, another kitchen, another bathroom. She rebuked herself for the way she curtailed them, objecting to the tough half-moons of cut toenail in the bottom of the bath, fastidious about his socks in the linen basket, silent for days at a time, funny about noise, various minor tyrannies.

'I'm sorry,' she said.

'It's only me that's going . . .' Patsy said. 'We're not going together.'

Willa stared at her. Didn't believe it. They got on fine. The way they joked, played cards, went for drives, argued. Patsy said it was all front. Said it was over, long ago. She'd written to Tom. Her mind was definitely made up.

'You need a little break from each other,' Willa said.

'There's someone else,' Patsy said, shy.

'I've never noticed,' Willa said.

'You were busy,' Patsy said.

'With glass,' Willa said, bitterly.

Patsy told her how they'd met, fallen, connived and come to their decision.

'Who's going to tell Tom?' Willa said.

'I thought you would,' Patsy said.

'I can't,' Willa said, very heartless, like a judge.

'I see,' Patsy said flattened. She should never have given in, the moment she opened her mouth to tell the truth she fucked it. What got into her at all – pity and

45

softness, all the currents inside you when you see your mother dead or someone sweating from hard work.

'I can't go on with Tom, it's disgusting that's what it is,' she said, to try and wring pity.

'It must be hard when you love someone else,' Willa said.

But Willa didn't understand, if she did she would say 'go'.

'It would be cruel not to tell him,' Willa said.

'I suppose it would,' Patsy said. As many kinds of cruelty as there are colours in the rainbow.

'You'll have to tell him, otherwise he'll never accept it.'

'He'll never accept it anyhow,' Patsy said, 'I know him.' Why was it that the minute you put your thoughts into action they went haywire? In your head you knew what to do but it never turned out like that. She burst into tears. Frustration, anger, disappointment. So many mixed-up feelings. She turned her head away and wiped her tears with her arm, as they came.

'I'll help you,' Willa said. Help. She was thinking 'Who now will protect me from Herod, who now will I turn to when that knock on the door, that ring, that tap on the shoulder catches up with me?' Even his face that had slipped out of her mind was slipping back in, his long-suffering icon face, his forehead high and pale, lineaments fixed in thought, an expression of pity that turned out to be merely self-pity.

'I'll do it myself,' Patsy said, resigned.

Willa said they should have a drink. She ran up the garden. Still running she entered the house through the sitting-room and from the corner cupboard got two best glasses. The wine was kept in a cooler place. She brought the old-fashioned corkscrew because Patsy liked being barmaid, putting a bottle between her knees and pulling with all her might. When she pulled the blood rushed to her cheeks.

'A job for you,' Willa said handing her the wine and the bent corkscrew.

But when Patsy pulled, tears ran down over the blood-reddened cheeks. She didn't want wine. Willa begged her to have some.

'Is he nice?' Willa asked, gently.

'He has red hair,' Patsy said. Why was she always the one to be sacrificed? When her mother brought home bachelors' shirts she had to wash them – spend hours over the tub; when she met Tom she worked with a crowd of girls and she wanted to stay like that for years, but he was on about a little flat and mightn't they as well be married as courting, and she gave in. Nice! The only nice thing in her whole life, lying down, standing up, premises without a stick of furniture, nice before, during and after, going around for days with a pain, the pain from having had him so much and the other pain of wanting him, more.

They raised glasses and saw each other for an instant rosy and happy through the pink liquid, but even as they drank they knew that the friendship had come to an end. Trust had gone out of their eyes. Now, they were different people.

'You can go next week,' Willa said.

'Yes, next week,' Patsy said absently. Even if she went now in spite of Willa they could trace her. She had blathered too much. Tom would find her. Another murder for next day's news.

'And you'll feel better about it then,' Willa said idiotically. Patsy smiled.

The sun shone very clear and on the red-stained cork the name of Portugal stood out.

A telegram was sent. Patsy had unpacked. It was as a beautiful family they sat down to dinner. Beef casserole. Orange peel in the sauce. Tom picked the bits of peel out first, then commenced to eat, ravenous.

'I stripped a room to the bare shell.

'Forty blokes under me and I'm fitter than any of them.

'Rooms have ribs like everybody else.

'Press my pants. I'm invited to a wedding.'

Tom talking. Tom's hour. Home from demolition, his feet sweaty, his hands washed, his eyes inclined to blink from the all-day shower of dust and mortar. His hair combed, the quiff in place, hair oil thick and runny upon it.

The hair oil glistened as the sun passed over his head. The hair itself had a glint of red.

'You have red in your hair,' Willa said.

'Jesus,' Patsy said, but to herself.

'If you grew a beard it would be red,' Willa said. Tom looked very pleased. He was interested in his appearance and Willa knew that. It was by his walk and by his hair that Tom most revealed himself. He walked with a swagger, that swagger that men in country dance halls affect when the music starts up and they go across the floor to proposition a girl. His hair he combed at odd moments throughout the day. He had bits of combs everywhere, broken bits of old combs.

'I had a good day,' he said. They were pulling a place down in the country. Fine house once. Plenty of tennis courts, lavatories with bowls shaped so that there was full evidence of achievement, lavatories disconnected of course, not that that impeded some of the lads; beautiful game preserve, able to catch pheasants with his bare hands. A week ago they had started and now the house was nearly down. Floor by floor, room by room, marvellous the way they pulled on rope and waited for it to crumble.

'We had a good day too,' Willa said. 'We painted the wall.' In fact they had done less than half of it. From the moment Patsy's news broke the work ceased and they were busy talking. Willa doing most of it. In the end Patsy went away to be by herself.

'White wedding,' Tom said and produced the invitation card. Little silver bells painted around the four corners, silver lettering, his name printed in capitals, all perfect except that the wedding was taking place in South Africa. He showed it to his wife. Her name was not on it.

Patsy looked but didn't say 'feck' or any of the usual things. She was silent, chewing her food, slowly, listlessly. Silent and fed up.

'You know . . . I think I cut the carrots wrong,' Willa said to humour her.

'So I see . . .' Patsy said gruff. Nothing would mend that breach.

Tom thought they must have had a tiff.

'What's up?' he said. Not that he minded. He was nearer to his wife when she and Willa were cool. Times he couldn't get a word in edgewise because of their confabulations. Times he came in from work and not a kettle, not a dish down and they looked at him like he had no right to come in. Let them be cool. A breakage most likely. Patsy had powerful hands. Wrenched glasses apart in the tea-cloth, just drying them.

'Severed, alas . . .' he said, delighted.

'Tell us your news,' Willa said, ignoring the mockery.

'Let me think if I have any.' He put a lot of food in his mouth, chewed scarcely at all, then smiled, and waved the fork. 'Oh yeh, they've given the go-ahead to the darkie's widow to sue.'

'Sue who?' Willa asked.

'Me, being as I'm foreman and was instrumental.'

But Patsy remained in her reverie, unamused, unprovokable.

'Another darkie today hit by jib, no witnesses, fortunately . . . they lack brain they do, all brawn I suppose.'

Willa was piqued. Another hint at Auro? They didn't like him coming, they kept barging into the sitting-room every so often with buckets of coal or fresh ice. Didn't want intruders. Anyone that might tip them out. Well it would be different now. Willa wondered how he would take it. If he might become violent, or cry, or get drunk for a week. She might have to call the police. A thing she had never done in her life. A shaming thing. It was not easy to eat, knowing all she knew, but she got on with it and pretended to be at her ease. Poor Tom, he had no notion yet. Poor Patsy thought it could be done for her, but it never can. Poor Willa, heading for a worse solitude.

'But they can't sue you, they must sue the boss,' Willa said.

'What do I care,' he said, laughing to himself. Patsy said what was so funny. He said he stood to win fifty quid if a horse came in on next day's race. Patsy said they heard that before. He said if they won they'd go to Paris, see the Follies.

'That's great,' said Patsy because she didn't believe

him. And again Willa's mind ran on to wretched scenes, and it seemed to her that she had been in the exact same situation once before although she knew very well that she had not been.

'They're still dying in Ireland,' she said, pointing to a letter that she had opened later in the day. It had been such a long day since Patsy made known her intentions. Willa read the paper – more catastrophe, molluscs that came with Napoleon's army soiling the lakes and jetties of Europe – had a walk, took three soluble aspirins and still found herself with two hours to dawdle through.

'Rope or sheep dip?' Tom said.

Bulletins of drastic death often reached them – men hanging from trees by courtesy of their own piece of horse rope, inferior Jesuses as Patsy once put it, found by anyone and everyone, but mostly by the poor postman, because foul deeds were done late at night and found first thing in the morning by the postman. Men with whippets, total abstinence badges, bachelors ulcer-prone, tough men from all over.

'No, a charmed death,' Willa said. She would tell them about the old woman who died. It would get them through dinner without any more collisions.

'She lived five fields away, from us,' Willa began. 'Kept her Mass shoes in a hedge, made a good rice pudding with raisins in it, wore a black coat down to her ankles, had broken rosary beads, prayed out loud in the chapel, prayed for the dead, her own dead – three daughters had galloping consumption – and the dead of others, was a martyr to shingles; all her life she wanted to go for a drive but never achieved it until the day of her death.'

'In the hearse?' Tom said, a bit of respect in his voice. Willa said no, told how the forester had come to buy the rights of the mountain, and how they had driven up a by-road to look at it and discuss price. Then when the woman got home she complained of feeling dizzy and asked to be brought out, then she lay under a tree and died. Willa said it was the only tree there.

She allowed herself to get carried away. Said the dizziness was surely more appropriate to young girls who dance too much on an empty stomach. She told them – they did not wish to know – that it was the only tree because the wind impaired the growing trees. Patsy wished to hell she'd stop raving. She told them about a spring well that had appeared magically at the base of that tree and then just as magically disappeared. Willa said that part of the countryside was founded on limestone and this, though valuable for crops, and great for rhododendrons, sucked in streams and rivers unaccountably. The schoolteacher had told them that there was a region in Yugoslavia with the exact same phenomenon. Tom said schoolteachers in Ireland knew their stuff. Then he told his wife for Christ's sake to make the tea. He liked his tea with the grub, not after.

'Best time to die when your wish is granted,' Willa said. Auro told her that the last thing a hanged man did was to ejaculate. A woman also? No point therefore in having holy oils smeared beforehand on the sinning zones – lids, nostrils, lips, palms, insteps. What did God have to say about that?

'There's worse ways of dying than under a tree,' Tom said. 'Forty ways alone of killing a man.'

'Here we go, back to Shitsville,' Patsy said out loud and nearly scalded herself, so hurriedly did she pour the water from the kettle. She wanted to get upstairs and get it over and done with. If she'd had her wits about her she'd be nearly there now. Diabolical.

'It's all in the technique . . .' Tom said, ignoring his

wife's outburst. He was in a mood for a chat. 'Hitler had the technique, Shakespeare, Stalin, a bone-setter at home had it . . .' No doubt Tom included himself in that illustrious list. Willa smiled but with sheer nervousness. People clung to being the thing they were not and that if brought too far was their undoing. Herod called himself a Jew but had none of a Jew's ways, and Herod's transplanted uncles, had they been Jews, would not be alive; as it was they survived the war and then with a million others were evicted as a reprisal. Admittedly they wanted to be Jews because one of Herod's uncles – a fiddler by profession – sawed his right hand off rather than serve the cause of nationalism. Expiators all! Herod punishing himself for a crime that he could not conceive of, Herod twice destroyed, not a German, not a Jew, a nothing. And she herself an accomplice in that destruction because she did not point out to him his mistake. She must tell Tom not to give himself false stature, she must tell him some other day.

*

Black City. Plenty of tall buildings but black, with soot. Pigeons discoloured too. Not grey or blue with the different shades over the breast. Sooted. Lads on the job against him because he was new. What did he care! He waited in the bar of the railway station and bought twenty cigarettes. On an ordinary day he rolled his own but they'd be nice to offer when she got in. Got her favourites. Plenty of people around but he kept to himself. A hardly-eaten sandwich on a plate that he kept his eye on. Hadn't a bite since lunch. He drank the beer in one gulp, not to show off but because he was thirsty. The day was unnaturally heavy. Waitress came and took the sandwich away. Crabbed. Bad marriage behind a thing like that. He smiled at his own joke.

His wife said Shropshire was the next worst thing to prison. But then she had no feeling for nature. None.

A few minutes before the train was due he went out and stood on the platform, half smiling to himself. She might be wearing a hat or something out of the ordinary. He felt she would either be first off the train, or last, being as she was involved in an adventure. His heart was pounding but trains always did that to him ever since he was small. If she had a heavy bag they'd get a taxi. But if she wanted they'd walk. He was disappointed that she wasn't first off. All the people looked crumpled, even people in good clothes. When loads of people had come through and he still waited he saw the porter walking from the very end of the train closing the doors as he walked. He went through the barrier and shouted to the porter that there was still someone on the train, but the porter said no. When they came close they had a heated argument about it and his stammer put him at a right disadvantage. They tried lavatories, the porter said 'Search all over if you want,' smug now that he was found to be in the right. No use searching the first-class cars. He tried those at the very back in case she had fallen asleep. The whole train was dark. She wasn't on it.

He went back to the bar and ordered himself a whiskey. A drunk came over to persecute him.

'Have you a wife?' the drunk said.

'I have,' Ron said, surly.

'I'm out one night a month and she's complaining,' the drunk said.

'I don't want to hear it,' Ron said.

'You have to, necessary data, they're a bugger they are . . .' the drunk said. Ron couldn't stand that, he rose, finished his drink, standing, and went home.

54

The telegram was waiting. The landlady in the hall waiting with it. He opened it. He read:

COMPLICATIONS AT THIS END. SEE YOU NEXT WEEK FOR SURE. BEST LOVE. PATSY.

He folded it up.
'Nothing wrong?' the landlady said.
'No,' he said. 'Just information.'
'Long ago we only got wires when people died,' she said.
'No one's died,' he said and climbed the stairs to his room. He sat on the bed and brought the loaf over, holding it in the crook of his arm as he cut it.

Bread knife made ripples over the butter as he spread it on bread. Reminded him of his eldest kid – funny drawings he did. Stones with faces, a woman half woman, half sewing machine. Only honest citizens – kids.

He didn't read the telegram over and over again. He wasn't that kind of man. One thing he hated was anyone trying to make a fool of him. Hated lies. Complications! Cold feet would be more like it. After he had eaten he took a pencil and sharpened it with the bread-knife. Hadn't begun to hurt yet. Like after having a tooth out and the jaw dead for hours. The wrench not felt at all. He'd feel it later but by then he'd have other troubles to think about. He pulled the letters from under the mattress and, looking for the one she'd written since he came, his eye fell on:

All that matters is that we love one another (Yes darling) Kisses and purfume (your kind).
I changed the furniture, always changing it (whimsicle).
Their ways are vile, fists, blows, fights, ours will be love, our daft love.

55

'Daft is right,' he said to himself as he rooted for the one he wanted, and read it carefully, a thing he hadn't done the morning he got it, so delighted was he.

Sorry about being in a state. Life is a cut-throat business. I trust you, its just that there are some very childish people in the world, in fact loads of them and when childish people get hurt they get nasty. Dont think you can beat them all the time, you cant.

That was the nub of it. Love-talk all eyewash. She wasn't serious. Peckham was a night out like going to the dogs or getting drunk. This was something she wasn't prepared for. Women had no pluck. A man would never break his word like that. Fine arrangement. In a black city with no one of his own. Lads on the docks dead against him because he was new. At least in Shropshire he could get away in the evenings, get out in the air and hear the birds. He knew what to say to her. Nothing bitter. He was galled but didn't let that show. He read the letter over and was pleased with it as being very restrained. Put a rubber band around her pile. Finding paper and twine was the hardest thing. He used the paper that was around the bread, it was a bit flimsy but it would do. The twine he had to wait until morning to get.

*

Tom was explaining the technique of impact to Willa. Demonstrated on a pencil. It broke in two. Said he could do the same thing with a wooden plank.

'We know, we know,' Patsy said. Night he did it in the pub Ron said, 'Your husband's a big man.' Nothing more.

'Hurry up,' Patsy said, unplugging the table light.

She said good night to Willa and Willa said good night back.

'Don't be so eager woman,' Tom said. He had business to discuss with Willa. Change of job. Willa and Patsy panicked in case he had heard something.

'They want me to be violence expert to a televison company.'

'There's no such job,' Willa said and smiled with relief.

He got to his feet, got her on her feet, raised his right hand, clenched the fist, talked rapidly. He talked about defunct types of X-ray machines. Then he talked about the nude woman on the wall and how she ought to have cupids around her holding the hair up. Willa said the nude woman was a disappointed person and had things on her mind other than cupids. While Willa was saying so he hit her on the nose hard. She put her hand up in an instinctive gesture of self-protection. Too late. He said exactly. He said that was what a violence expert was for. To teach actors to get the victim off guard, the way he got her. He did it in slow motion. Blood ran on to her fingers.

'What you do is have your hand raised, get the bloke involved in conversation and wham . . .'

Only then he noticed that her nose was bleeding and he drew back, apologizing. Patsy put the second light back on. She said he was an ignorant bastard. Willa sat down and held her head back. She drank her tea and in the rear of her throat the blood taste got mixed up with the taste of tea.

'You shouldn't have gone and done that,' Patsy said.

'Did,' Willa said, in her mind, out of habit.

Tom put the car keys at the back of Willa's neck and kept apologizing. When it stopped bleeding she sat up and held a handkerchief to her nostrils just in case. Tom

57

said did she want driving anywhere. She shook her head. She wanted to be alone. For the second time she and Patsy exchanged good nights, and Willa winked cheerfully in order to give her a little courage in what she had to do.

Rain. From the sitting-room Willa looked out at it. Thin rain, wrapping itself round things: the tool shed, the flowers, the flower stalks, wrapping itself round these things like a winding sheet. It had to rain. A child of nine, one of her favourite people, wrote it all down for her and presented it to her on a jotter. His hands decked out with cheap rings. A ring for each finger. He got them instead of pay when he worked at the fun fair, small boy of nine, one of her favourite people, able to humour her, 'Got this for you Willa, did this for you Willa, wrote this for you Willa.'

And she read:

Clouds are made of tiny drops of water. It is this that makes them float. The clouds float because the tiny drops of water take longer to come down than something solid. The drops are so small that a million would cover a penny. Do you know why the clouds are always there? Well, it's because when it rains water comes down. Then it turns into vapour and rises to a cloud. You can sometimes see this happening. First you see a thin wisp of cloud and slowly it grows bigger. In 1931 Professor Piccard rose in a steel ball to 53,000 feet. He discovered a lot about clouds. There are three kinds of clouds.

1. Cumulus which are heaped up clouds.
2. Cirrus which are streaks of clouds.
3. Stratus which are flat clouds.

Small boy of nine, one of her favourite people in all the world. His arms thin as sticks. Why did his arms break her heart so? Their utter, utter starvation because, and his little genitals so slack and his skin flaky after the bath, the flakes like talcum dust so white. She took care of him the time his mother had a breakdown. 'What do you want?' she asked, after she had bathed him. Thought he would say 'Cocoa in bed,' but he said 'You to be my Mum,' and she put a low knot in the soft sash of his pyjamas and carried him in to bed, but when his mum got better she sent him home again. Always sent people home: small boy of nine, Auro, Patsy, Tom, always gave so much and then drew back fearful of the eternal responsibility of them. All except Herod. She should be with them now upstairs, helping them to get through their biggest crisis, she should be refereeing, she should be telling Tom about the hidden meanings of the heart, she should be bolstering them for this hour when all the other hours of their life were being squeezed into the one savage scene, but no she was downstairs in her twilight world drinking whiskey. She intended to get drunk, to slide into that irresponsible if joyless state. What are you? she thought. A person who does not love her country, a person who cannot love a man, a person without child who babbles on about love. In a way she envied dwarfs. Had she ever done the difficult thing in her life? Do it, she said. Save them. Get up and do it. But she drank another whiskey and looked out at the thin rain. Up along the lawn was the track of white that occurred when Patsy walked away cursing, the wet brush in her hand, the wet brush dripping with paint. She drank the whiskey and crept upstairs to listen outside their door. Television was on and they seemed to be talking. No use intruding on them if Patsy hadn't yet told him. She couldn't hear a word because of the television. What was going on in there? Their ways so strange, so remote to her. She wandered from one room to another, in a pathetic round of the house. She should fill those rooms. No shortage of applicants. Once a car-load of Indians stopped to ask her about rooms. All men. She counted them by their turbans. They looked treacherous, huddled together in that small car asking for accommodation. She said that she was a stranger herself. Going from room to room – six in all – she closed windows. Rain had come in but nothing worse. Rain discolouring the parquet floor under the windows. In years to come those stains would be there – though deeper – and she could tell someone about a certain night when she saw a little of the disfiguration happen. At least she was getting to know the secrets of her house and its slow deterioration even if she did not know its inmates. People said that nervous breakdown showed in those who stared at a button for hours on end. She could well believe it.

On the way down she listened again and thought they were arguing but could not be sure. She had a mad notion to knock and invite them for champagne, but common sense re-established itself. Down in the sitting-room at one touch of a cord the curtains, like rivers, began to flow, runners ran smoothly over well-oiled rails, the curtains met, red velvet shut out the garden gloom and in the deep folds that red was densened and multiplied, so that the room had bouquet. She turned on all lamps, added whiskey to her glass, and sat down, minute in black, as though to act out her sorrow.

*

Tom got down on his knees to his wife. Called her darling. Called her 'Baggie', his private name for her. That was how it took him. They would do anything she wanted. He would pack up the job, they could go to

South Africa, put money on a house, anything, just she name it. He said he loved her and no one could kill that. He said to remember the day at the seaside, how happy they were, in her knickers, waves coming in over her and the knickers blown out with water. How they laughed. The way she lay on the water like one of the seals. How he loved her. Did she realize that? She said there were things in life she did not understand and love was one of them. He said, 'Say you love me.' She couldn't. He said 'Baggie,' very pleading. He said, 'Say you'll always love me,' and when she didn't he stood up and hit her very forcefully on the right cheek and for a second she was stunned. Then she said it was just as good for him that she didn't have her glasses on.

'I'll kill him, you know I'll kill him,' he said, pulling her up by the hair, then he put his hands around her neck, thumbs pressing on her Adam's apple. She couldn't speak, she couldn't swallow very well, she had to listen.

'Till he's nothing but pulp pulp and ululation you can have his brains as a souvenir me and you was gettin' along all right what he don't know is that his hours are numbered and no come-back I have my methods take that smirk off your fizz lettin' you outside the door was the mistake money for corsets well nobody fouls me for long oh no boy you discussed us with him our private life me and him in a race where did ye do it in the street like dogs every new broom sweeps clean you had the gall to offset my technique against his in the dogshit wakening me up in the middle of the night I'd say you're not right when you think it over you can't be right sailing out the front door leave me with a television licence and a load of dirty washin' so he's the bloke plays darts dirty hound I'll tell his widow, I'll tell her no one fucks my marriage up, where did you say he lived the sooner we get it over . . .'

All the while he had been talking she tried freeing her neck but to no avail.

'Answer me,' he said, releasing the grip.

'How the hell can I answer you when you're throttling me.'

'Nothing to what you will be, nothing to what you will be . . .'

He walked around shaking his hands as if there were drops of water on them. Relaxing his hands. Preparing for the next round.

'Get your clothes off, get in your birthday suit,' he said.

'I thought you was going to Peckham to kill him.'

'We have business to do first,' he said. 'Here I am,' and he opened buttons and took down his pants.

She stood quite still, not knowing how she was going to impede him. Great sudden tears came pouring down her face. He saw them and hope came in his eyes at his victory.

'You heard me,' he said. He was prancing about like an athlete.

'Oh for fuck's sake,' she said and put her hand over her eyes to try and make everything blank.

'Are you afraid?' he said.

'It's disgustin' that's what it is,' she said and he broke into a loud voice and began to hit her until she no longer knew what was happening. She didn't duck or anything. She just knew it was something he had to do. Then he removed as much of her clothing as was necessary, and her head was spinning and she did not very much care.

They were in bed when the doorbell rang. She tried

63

to worm her way out under. She thought of the horse she had to crawl under once but this was worse.

'I better answer that,' she said.

'You'll answer nothing,' he said.

'Willa is frightened of the door at night,' she said.

'Willa my arse,' he said.

She never knew he could be that cruel.

*

The doorbell had gone a few times before Willa ventured to answer it. She thought that Tom or Patsy might but neither of them did. The letter box was pushed in and issuing through the hall was a whistle. She opened it, and gladly let him in.

He carried a fur coat over his arm.

'I'm glad to see you,' she said, understating it. Auro said nothing, he just smiled and followed her through to the room. It was the same comfortable room and he was glad to be back.

'Look at me,' he said.

She drew away from him. Always when they met she had to keep moving around to control her initial flutteriness.

'I came to see if you're all right,' he said.

Oh the loving, the binding promise, the complicity that she attached to that little sentence.

He shook the coat that was on his arm to rid it of creases. 'Been trapping for you,' he said.

It was a white fur coat with enormous irregular black patches. The fur was long and hairy and the patches were like great eyes. He walked towards her, waving it as an enticement.

'Was that why you came?' she asked and thought it must also be an answer to her prayer.

'Yeh, to see how you're gettin' on . . .' He didn't

say I missed you, he didn't say you have echo, he didn't say a man has many a taste-bud, though all of these things would have been true. He couldn't say 'Beryl wouldn't talk, Beryl wouldn't cook, Beryl wouldn't screw.'

He waved the coat at her, swaying as he walked, pursuing her down the length of the long room until she got behind the curtains into the bay of the window where of course he cornered and caught her. She withdrew into the coat, not putting her arms in the sleeves but squirming inside the silken lining, inside the embrace of his arms, her chin on the hairy collar, feeling its softness, her cheek stroking his, his voice saying how glad he was to be back. In a whisper. Her purr. Safe, safe, inside his arms, inside the coat, inside the bay of the window. The alacrity of his hands as he shook it free in direct contrast with their stillness when they came around her. He still wore the bracelet and the ring that he said signified nothing but kept women away.

'There is no dinner left,' she said.

'We'll go out.'

'I've eaten one.'

'You'll eat another,' he said and put her arms into the sleeves and kissed her all the way to the door, she walking backwards, he walking in front, but his mind applied to kissing. Twice they bumped into the staircase.

'Just a minute,' she said and she ran upstairs to tell Patsy.

Their light was out and when she tapped Tom asked what she wanted.

'I'm going out for a while,' she said feebly.

'We're in bed.'

Not a meek out of Patsy.

*

In the dark the coat showed up strangely. There were no stars and the street light had defaulted. The coat showed up like an animal, with a life of its own and giant watchful eyes.

'A tundra animal,' she said. Not that she had ever seen one.

'Goat,' he said, 'or pied ponies.' She thought of patient goats tethered to gates and ponies in wastelands of rain, frenzied, and running about.

'Dappled,' she said.

'Like black men.' He tucked the coat around her knees as he shut her into the motor car.

Was Beryl black?

*

In the restaurant she kept it on. The sleeves were too long and dipped into her soup but that didn't matter. She did not say 'Why won't Beryl have it?' nor did she yield to pettiness and say 'Does Beryl still have the little come-hitherish lisp?' She said,

'I hope it's lucky.'

'It is,' he said. 'It suits you, and that's lucky.'

They were drinking water and when he realized this he called for the waiter, loudly.

'London water,' he said. 'Drunk first in Reading, flushed in Reading, seweraged in outer Essex, filtered in a bed and re-served in King's Road Chelsea to regular customers. Bloody scandalous.' The waiters knew him and had come round to listen. It was not often or at least not always that he was so expansive.

They had champagne. He stirred it in the glasses with a fork and said 'Wish.' She wished for nothing more than a nice evening.

In restaurants she always thought of Herod because it was in a restaurant they met. On a day in spring or perhaps a winter masquerading as spring. She worked three hours an afternoon and he came again and again, the mongrel with the mongrel talent and brown hair that was combed and brought forward; and then after days of silent wooing he said,

'How long is it since your breath smelt clean?' And those words of such startling simplicity started them off. She looked at Auro and the black fleece of his hair. She said, 'Don't ever have your hair brought over your forehead.'

'Why not?'

'I don't like it, I think the person might be fanatic.'

He laughed.

'You can't put it down to a haircut.'

'You can't but you do,' she said. And then she smiled at him.

'Look, tell me something simple that is not about either of us.'

'Like what?' He gave her back a smile.

'Like that in a square in central London the ground-floor windows are dark at night and the upper floors have lights scattered here and there, the ground floors are offices and upstairs there are a few bed-sitters. I like knowing that, I don't know why.'

'I do.'

'Why?'

'Because it is something simple that is not about either of us.' They laughed. It was a night when they would have laughed at anything.

' "In case of emergency break glass, unlatch door," written in the Underground,' he said.

'Great things in the Underground,' she said, hedging. Was he resorting to symbols on one glass of champagne? 'Invitation to see Carlyle's clothing and a place with plastic snow that has something like the feel of firm snow.'

'That's what you want me to do,' he said, 'break glass, unlatch door.' She shook her head and said yes and no in the same instant.

'How've you been?' he asked then. He would have liked it to be resolved for her but he still wanted to be first. Her timidity gave him a special type of thrill and each time he saw her he liked her that much more.

'I've been all right.' She was going to tell him about Patsy and Tom but first she was going to enjoy him.

'What about you?' she said.

'I was in Madrid, on a job. Chattin' up a bird one night, best Spanish, Señorita and all that. "Are you pot or something?" she said, "I'm British."'

'And the chimpanzee is pulling levers in outer space,' she said.

She tasted his food, he tasted hers, they took no notice of those who came or went, they were at a corner table, content with one another.

'Any discoveries?' he asked, half in joke.

'Yes. Do you know why clouds are always there?'

'Is there a catch in it?' He was in no mood for a sad story and Willa was a mine of them.

'It's a good story,' she said.

'Save it.' He meant for bed.

Was he taking her home? Of course. *And* tucking her up in bed.

'Just lie beside you,' he said, the time-worn entrance tab used by many a man to get into many a hesitant girl's cave.

'We'll tell good stories,' she said.

'All right.'

'Whisper them.'

'Shout them.' He hip-hip-hurrahed but no one took any notice.

'I won't ask if you love me more or less than the others,' she said.

'More,' he said.

'I won't ask if you love me at all,' she said, but already she had begun to be nervy. Her voice was several pitches higher. She said disconnected things. Couldn't they play chemmy being as it was her lucky day, or go to Covent Garden and buy onions, or wait for the hotel to open that served eggs benedict for breakfast? He said no to all those things. He said:

'Sluice gates must come down.' He paid the bill and guided her between the tiny tables out the narrow passage to the door. The table had check cloths and were like draught boards.

'People could play draughts here,' she said. She was saying anything that came into her head.

And so it went on, in fits and starts all night – the violence, the wrangling, the 'come for a drive', the quiet bouts, the threats, the crying like a child. Made her do a certain thing she had never done before. Turned out to be the worst of all because her stomach felt sick anyhow and she thought she would vomit. Vile. Vile taste. When she heard the car coming back and heard them getting out and laughing she said, 'Better kill me quick, they're back,' and for a minute it looked as if he might, but he just threw a dish at the wall and laughed as it flew into pieces.

'That's Royal Crown Derby,' she said.

'Royal Crown Smithereen,' he said, still laughing.

'They'll hear you.'

'The nigger and the whore, beauty and the beast,' he said, still laughing.

She never knew he could be that desperate.

He opened the door to call them, to let them know, to let Willa know that nobody was going to mess him around. But when he opened the door he said nothing at all.

'Close the door,' Patsy said.

After a while he did and when he got back into bed he cried, they both cried, but separate.

*

Auro had not seen the brass bed because it was new.

She had bought it in her longing to be prepared for him. Along with a stock of nightdresses, a man's razor, and contraceptive jelly. He said he had reason to believe that he had been born in a brass bed. She said did he ever see his mother. He said no. She said hers died of a liver complaint. Father too. He said they were quits then.

'You know what,' she said, 'you stop blaming your parents the day you realize that you are an uglier person than the you they let loose on the world.'

'Hush, hush,' he said and opened the buttons of her nightdress. They opened easily. She'd undressed in the bathroom. He put his nose to her flesh, smelt it, breathed through it, came up for air, listened to her heart beats, kissed her, itched his nose on her breast, asked why she shivered, lit a cigarette, put it in her mouth, asked why she cried.

'It's too late, it was already too late when you came.'

'Don't tell me you are too old.'

'You do one or two wrong things in your life and you are crippled – no matter how many right things it is those one or two wrong things.'

'Wrong doesn't come into it.'

'Not now, but maybe it would later.'

'What do you think I am?' he asked.

'I don't know what you are. You never know another person until you give yourself up to them.'

'You make it sound like jail.'

'It is.'

'You mean it was.' He said it softly and with solicitude. He looked at her face, trying to deduce from it the muddle that was holding her back. He said,

'One of those drunken Irishmen with the traditional safety pins on the trousers' fly?'

She shook her head.

'They never touched me. I never went that near.'

'Then who, who harmed you?'

'Someone who said he would save me from falling over a cliff.' One day she would acquit herself. She would give him the letters. Let him have the whole Herod Saga, the tale of the love that was to be so wholesome, the love that led to madness.

'We all pick losers, we're all on the run from some mistake.'

'Of course . . . ' she said. There was no point in going on. To tell him a little would only convey a fragment of the menace and to tell him the whole story would send him home in disgust. Tragedy had lost its importance. Anyhow, who wanted a patient?

'You like me, I can tell.'

'I like you,' she said, weary.

'And you want me?'

'I don't want anyone.' What he took to be excitement and desire was just a hysteria of the flesh, a rash breaking out inside. It did not have much to do with him. It did not have enough to do with him. To assuage it he was not necessary. She heard Herod's laugh in her head. It was the opposite to an echo. It began faintly, got louder and louder like a laugh travelling up a hallway. Auro might not laugh, might not even blame her, but would certainly vanish.

'You might feel let down,' she said.

'I might, or you might feel let down.'

They heard a scream and a door being banged. She jumped out of bed.

'Who is there?' he said off-hand, and answered, 'Ah, very good, show the girls in . . .'

'There's trouble with Patsy and Tom,' she said. 'She's leaving him but he doesn't know yet.'

'I could have told him that,' he said, and she thought

by his voice that his temper was souring a little and she didn't wonder.

Back in bed she said, 'It's another reason why I'm on edge,' but he shook his head and said it wasn't. She might like to think it was but he knew different. He said he would tell her a story called Cat in Spain. He said, 'A cat in the sun lying on her side with the male fucking her, lying on her side indifferent, the way she'd lie after her dinner, one male fucking her and a whole circle of males around looking on, waiting for their chance, but it was no use, the female didn't want it.'

'I try,' she said. 'I do try.'

'Your mistake is you measure everything beforehand.'

'I didn't always,' she said, 'I didn't always.'

He whistled between his teeth, he whistled quite happily. Soon he would put on his jacket and go. And, as often before, they had started an evening but not finished it: it could only be finished in bed. Now they were guarded people again, destined for different breakfasts, separate thoughts.

'Why do you bother?' she said.

'I don't want you to end up like one of those women along the King's Road carrying a brown-paper parcel.'

'What's in those brown-paper parcels?'

'Nothing,' he said. 'More brown paper.'

She did not want to end up like that at all. She had a mortal dread of it. Standing outside the auctioneer's windows, her dismay when she saw a paraffin heater with a pair of lady's shoes before it, placed as they might be if there were feet in them, the toes turned up at the tips from over-heat, and in that little grim tableau she foresaw her later life, spinster nights before a fire, shoes turning up with heat.

They held hands but it was courtesy holding. Always

at first their hands met in welcome, then tightened in passion, wrestled with one another, and when it became dangerous she rebuffed his, leaving a little more hurt, a little more quandary, each time. Soon he would give up altogether.

'What would *you* do if you were a woman?' she said.

'I'd have babies all the time and feel sorry for myself,' he said.

'You wouldn't.'

He put his jacket on. The lovely speckled shades she would not know. He said he might be going to Canada on a picture. She thought that sort of news always comes at the wrong moment. He said he'd telephone her though. She wanted to see him out. He said the nightdress would scandalize milkmen. But she insisted. As if a miracle would occur on the way down. He went out the path whistling, kicking a stone ahead of him. No resentment when he turned round and jerked his head sharply by way of good-bye. He was always doing neck jerks and keeping himself fit. No resentment.

The rain had sweetened the air. Why can't women walk alone at night? She looked for the stars but there were none.

*

The reproduction bed was what she was left with and the first wild shafts of grief that always hit her when she let him go away like that, empty. Rungs in which she could see herself, lines on the blue ceiling, almost but not quite glossed over with paint, the electric lamp crackle; always the same, her worldly goods and her thoughts. Each time when he left she thought that if he were to come back her fears would have vanished. But each time she believed it less. You can't, she said. You may clean the hand-basin with the hand-towel. You may put a dream of frost in glass. You may induce orgasm with the heel. You may cross the road at the right moment or cross it at the wrong moment and choose to get killed. You may lose weight by declining bread, potatoes, spaghetti, all the mother foods that your soft, weak, unchewing nature craves for. Cow, without cow's wisdom, without a cow's ruminativeness. You cannot do the one thing that would take you out of aspic, out of your dungeon, away from limbo.

Near dawn she went down to get herself some hot milk. Not rosy, not aureate yet, only the hour of chill. Met Tom en route. Explained that she was on the way to get hot milk. Her quick breathing gave her away.

'You know something?' he said, as he stopped to let her pass on the stairs.

'No,' she said, with little inclination to talk.

'I thought I heard burglars.'

'It was my friend going out.'

'Great exhaustion tonight,' he said, 'supplying women.'

She pretended not to understand. He put out his hand but did not touch her.

'Very nice garment, is that in the mode now?'

She drew the robe around her front and clutched at the collar as she went on down.

'There are five breeds of salmon but only one leaping salmon, swims hundreds of miles upriver from the sea to lay eggs, when eggs are hatched descends the rivers again, back to sea . . .'

She thought he must be going mad and turned to look. He was reading from the paper and she pitied him then because she knew how desperate it must be, reading at that hour. But she did not let her pity show because there was nothing she could do about his trouble. He went on reading and out of politeness she listened . . .

'After two years or more they return to the river to

breed and make a second attempt to the sea. Survival again is two per cent,' he said. He read like a child.

'Hazards,' he said. She went on down.

'I'll assist you,' he said and followed her.

She did not want that at all.

She held the saucepan, pressing it on the gas flame to make it boil faster. He got out a tray and a tray-cloth. He laid it with a flourish.

'Catholics please note, selected fish course available on Fridays,' he said. They saw that once. Didn't she remember? In one of the posh places she brought him and Patsy to. Patsy not able to eat the steak because it was full of pepper. Ordered sandwiches.

No, she didn't remember.

'Ah, gala times,' he said, a terrible drop in his voice. She picked up the tray and hurried out.

'I'll have it in bed,' she said.

'If it was my brother-in-law he'd join you.'

A tight shave. She went up those stairs in a flash.

*

Next day Patsy did not show her face at all. Tom brought the meals up and Willa did not know how much or how little he had been told but he acted tempestuously and kept his dressing-gown on and kept apologizing for it. She looked in once, Tom was by the bed playing patience, Patsy in bed, her cheeks as mauve as the nightdress she wore. One of Willa's. One worn in one of her failures with Auro and promptly given away to reduce shaming memories.

'Are you all right?' she said to Patsy.

'I'll be fine on Monday,' Patsy said. Not a signal passed between them. Tom sat there like a watch-dog. Willa saw the bits of broken china all over the floor. Patsy immediately said there must have been a storm.

Willa said it did not matter and wished she hadn't been caught looking. She brought in her coat then, to show it. She didn't fit it on. She just carried it in. Patsy said it was like what Russians wore.

'You'll have to insure it,' Patsy said. Willa didn't think so as it was goat.

'Yes, it's goat,' Tom said, feeling it along the hem. Nobody contradicted him. Nobody had the spirit.

On Monday Tom did not go to work. The excuse was that Patsy had to go to the doctor. She said she was going alone, she wanted fresh air. They had an argument about it, out loud in the kitchen. Willa was pleased to learn that some of her old spirit had returned. Patsy was not the torpid mauve victim that lay in Saturday's bed, inert as a fish on the shore. Patsy was fighting back.

'I'm going myself,' she said, defiant.

'Then go,' Tom said.

'There's car insurance this week, you go to work,' she said.

'I'll think it over,' he said, but he didn't go.

He sat in the kitchen and put pennies under paper and scratched out the design of each penny on the paper. Willa walked about with the fur coat on. It was not cold but she was undecided as to what to do. She daren't go to her studio. She wanted to be disagreeable so that he would go to work. She hated him now. He was another of the ones that put love on a leash. She wanted to say something cutting to him, something that would get him out of their sight. When the doorbell rang he rushed to answer it, as if he was expecting someone.

'Is there a Josephine O'Dea here?' he called in from the hallway.

'You know there isn't,' Willa said peevishly.

Shortly after he came back to the kitchen with a parcel.

'Oh God,' Willa said, seeing a flimsy package held together with coarse twine and uneven clusters of red sealing wax, 'now we'll have to send it back.' Small inconveniences infuriated her.

'All right, all right, we'll send it back,' he said, pacifying her. With his hands he pulled the cord down. She had a premonition of disaster a second before the contents fell through the flimsy paper and Patsy's letters tumbled all over the table. He grabbed some, she grabbed others. They were on ruled paper, on the backs of bills, on Willa's headed notepaper with Willa's name crossed out.

'Caught red-handed,' he said and began to read quickly, fiendishly, going from one to the other as if his eyes were not moving fast enough for what his mind was ready to absorb.

Willa looked at the first one in her hand, it was stained with egg, she read:

How about our cums.
I shook you with my little ball of feathers in oil – it's Eastern that.
It's so Big. My hands are getting hard but I put cream on them.

It was like a letter written at odd moments throughout the day, as indeed was probably the case.

No one hears our prayers. We talk about nutty things. We may not be perfect but we are perfect for each other. What love can do. Are we sadists? You know the bit I mean with the flex. w–h–a–c–k.

'Listen to this, listen to this,' Tom said and read out, ' "I don't give twopence for his car now and I have no interest in driving lessons. He says there are forty ways of killing a man but it's all front, believe me. Now my dear Ron I'm going to say a serious word to you and

don't laugh. Say a prayer he'll go down the country,"'
and then he stopped reading and said, 'Christ, it's not
front now . . .' He stopped talking and read another.

Willa felt sick with terror.

Would I live with you, not half. What do you think I brought
the green nightdress along for. That policeman doesn't
know what he missed. If he saw you, if I saw it myself. Bring
mirrors. I'm only joking. Do what you want. I'm not
blocking you (not half).

Tom was cursing and laughing and crying all at once.
Willa pitied him now and did not know how to control
him.

'How's that?' he said, handing her another. It was
daubed where his spit or his tears had dropped on the
ink.

How would you like me in a topless or something. You're a
caution wanting pink briefs. I never wore briefs before. I wish
I could get you a present you'd like. I never really have to
think what to write to you, I never run out, its amazing, I
could write and write and write. It must be love. Do me a
'No entry' sign to keep him out will you? Is that nasty.
No using your tongue, no wringing it. Ha Ha.

Her first thought was that they ought not to be reading
them, they were too private, too telling and too beautiful
for any but the one they were addressed to. Her next
thought was that there were at least three dozen little in-
cendiary bombs on the kitchen table, and that Tom must
be prevented from seizing them. She gathered the ones
that were lying around. She scanned the letter in another
handwriting that had come with them. In this whirl of
discovery Ron had been ignored as if he were not important to Tom's investigation. The letter was flat, it
spoke of his wife, his children and the mistake of those
who made promises lightly.

'They won't do you any good,' she said, taking some others from Tom.

'Christ,' he said, 'they're invaluable,' and he took them back at the same moment as he read another.

Funny about us both dreaming of white rats. Dark fur is more common but dreams are strange. I suppose it was Willa's rugs.

'We're all in it,' he said, 'we're all in it.' He wanted her to become indignant too.

'But it's over, over,' Willa said.

'Ah, there'll be turbulence,' he said and held up another. He couldn't stop. He was like a child who had just discovered the pleasure of reciting before an audience.

He said he wanted to look into the libel aspect as well as all else.

Time dont matter – I've figured it all out. Last night in bed I was lying nearly asleep and I kissed you goodnight and suddenly you was with me really and I held you and I said 'I love you,' (we kissed) 'You're beautiful' (and we kissed) 'Darling will you give me a baby' and we kissed and made love and you said 'Of course I will.' . . .

He had got so caught up in his fury that he did not notice Willa sneak away. She went out the hall door, drawing it until the latch grazed the lintel, then putting the key in the lock and turning it quietly. Thief-like. Poor Tom. He would kill someone.

*

Willa waited at the bus stop. It was a gamble but she waited all the same. Tom might come first. Nowhere to hide. A street of little shops, little factories – castings, welding, stationery. She went in the doorway of the pub named after a tree and each time a car came she made as if to go into the pub but it was closed. She started to walk. Afraid of Tom and suddenly unaccountably certain of Herod's reappearance. Panic always brought him back. She could hear his voice, 'You were about to betray me.' That too calm voice with the idiosyncrasy in the pauses. It was by the pauses one knew that Herod had learnt English late in life, and by the one word 'mine'. 'Mine own, mine comrade, mine God.' If Tom drew up she would say she was having a walk, he could do nothing to stop her. Yes, she was trembling, but behind that there was something worse. There was regret. She should have let Patsy go in the first place. What had made her act like that? Stupidity, she felt, and selfishness and fear. She needed them as guardians, it was why she employed them in the first place, and she expected that they would stay for ever. The one thing she forgot was that they might have storms of their own. The same Patsy in an apron that scrubbed and on Sunday took it off and played cards, the same Patsy that got red when she drank port wine was able to say,

'Tell me we was meant for each.'
'I think we'll both die of a broken heart.'
'Friday night, pulling your shoes off, like rabbits, the water burnt out of the kettle, a whistling kettle mind you!'

Lines from them hit her with their honesty, their love. They would hit her for the whole of her life. In that she had meddled, she the great soloist about love. The Patsy she thought she knew was only a fraction of the person. This was the woman that hour by hour held her own thoughts back while nursing Willa in her monologues. If only she'd come. Perhaps she'd gone in by one of the other streets that led into their road. Willa thought of the dream she'd had where the two men were knifing her, and how laughable it was now compared with the real drama, on her hands. She waited. Read advertisements. Superlative adjectives. Posters making claims for three different brands of cigarettes and one for brown bread that carried photographs of caviare and cucumber but no bread. The chip shop closed for decorating. One brick chimney puffing smoke, a chimney not much higher than the factory wall, a watch dog behind a gate, his tits hard and formidable like the barbs on the wall wire. On a 'Vacancies For' board a request for lady machinists. Monday morning, the world going on, lorries being towed, meals on wheels, foreigners in astrakhan hats, and Patsy in danger of her life.

*

As Patsy rose to get off the bus Willa jumped on the platform.

'Stay where you are,' Willa said loudly. Her jumping on like that created annoyance because passengers had not got off.

They sat in the back seat.

'Letters of yours came,' Willa said, unexpectedly shy. She had brought as many as she could. She wanted to say something approving, like that they were lovely, but she knew how irrelevant that was.

'What has he to say for himself?' Patsy asked, unruffled.

'Oh wife, children, duty,' Willa said.

'Ah he's got the guilts, he's got the diarrhoea,' Patsy said, and for a second Willa expected that they would be asked to get off the bus because the conductor, who was male, was standing over them.

'Well he'll have another mouth to feed,' Patsy said. Willa said impossible. Patsy said impossible but still true. Willa thought that as in a melodrama too many events were taking place within a short space of time.

'So I'm in the shithouse more ways than one,' Patsy said, laughing despite.

All the conductor wanted was their fares. Patsy showed him her old ticket and Willa handed him sixpence. Where were they going? Willa said to a taxi rank further up the road. Willa had it all planned. Patsy would go to her man, live with him, Willa would help in every way, Willa would talk to Tom, mislead him, appease him and finally make him come to terms with it. Willa would serve the cause of love.

'He needn't know about the pregnancy for a while . . .' she said.

'He knows, the doctor rang him,' Patsy said.

So he already paced the floor adding to the goriness of his intended crime.

'Why?' Willa said.

''Cause it could be his,' Patsy said and winked. 'Good news week?'

Willa had great admiration for someone in whom love, appetite, dream and deceit were all of a piece. She asked nothing more about the doctor or how thorough the examination had been. Always in awe of pregnant women she now felt something more, she wanted to mark the occasion above and beyond the squalidness of it so that Patsy would say ever after 'Me and Willa on a bus such and such a day and guess what she did.' But all she managed to say was, 'Where is he from?'

'He's a Kerry tiger,' Patsy said and reddened.

It was an incoherent time.

They got off the bus.

*

Willa gave her some money and then on an impulse, or

rather to convey the admiration that she had always hidden, she took off the Auro coat and gave it too.

'Jesus,' Patsy said.

'It's to bring you luck,' Willa said.

'You don't expect me to go in furs,' Patsy said, but quietly. When Patsy was grateful her voice took on an incredible gentleness. She took off her own coat and got into it. She put her hands in the pockets straight away. She felt at home in it, she beamed.

And they parted like that, Patsy inside the coat, round and safe and a little excited, Willa with her hand up in the arrested gesture of farewell, not able to say anything at all.

She took a taxi home. Tom was waiting at the gate. He had shaved and had put a good suit on.

'Where is she?' he said.

'Gone,' Willa said. Irrationally pleased at their victory.

'I'll find her,' he said. Then he noticed that she was in her dress and he said, 'In your coat! I'll spot her a mile away.'

She was on her way into the house to get some money for the taxi but he insisted on making her a present of it, of the fare, and he paid the driver who, naturally, thought they were both mad.

That afternoon Willa had the lock changed.

*

In the evening she waited in her sitting-room. The small boy of nine sat opposite. She thought of calling in other people but it was the small boy of nine she called in the end because she did not have to explain so much. The change in the room was already apparent. Glasses lying around, ashtrays full, the metal caps of bottles – from her tonic water and his Coca-Cola – on the floor where they had flown off in the opening, the Sunday papers unfolded. They played Monopoly. The seconds were ticked by faithfully on the grandfather clock.

'Say something, say anything,' she said to the small boy.

'When I go on a journey I always count the animals,' he said. He was winning. The doorbell alarmed her even though she had been waiting for it to ring.

'Now remember,' she said to the boy. He had been cued by her to move around, slam a door, make plenty of of noise, give the illusion that the house was full of people.

'Well?' she said when she opened the hall door, her face already fixed in a mask of annoyance.

'Have you got a moment?' Tom said, awkward now that he had come back. He had come earlier and tried his latchkey, and then he had gone away and got reinforcement. She had watched him from their upstairs window. He began to introduce his two friends but was cut short by her.

'I can't help you,' she said.

'All we're asking is where is she?' one of them said.

'I don't know, and I purposely don't want to know,' Willa said crisply.

'You put wrong ideas into her head,' Tom said. It was not like something he had just thought of, it was an opinion he had turned over often in his mind.

'Maybe I did,' she said.

'There's what's serious and there's what's fatal,' he said. Neither of his blokes spoke. They seemed shocked by her. Was it her thinness? Or the suede dress several inches above the knees? At any rate they looked harmless.

'I'm with someone now,' Willa said. It was such a

fatal sentence that she wanted to apologize for it. From within the realms of the house the men heard noise, footfall and a door being closed. A perfect decoy. Still they stood. She closed the door on them, from the inside she listened.

'God Almighty I built this bloody house, it was falling down,' Tom said. She wanted to open the door and say yes, and confirm the depth of his bitterness. But she went back to the room where the boy of nine was taking the thin spindly refills from a multicoloured Biro pen.

'What are you doing that for?' she said.

'Something to do,' he said, forlorn. There was a long evening ahead of them.

*

When Tom came again it was after midnight. He begged to be let in. For five minutes to get his sleeping suit. She would have to have been made of stone to refuse. The small boy of nine was upstairs asleep. She was forcing herself to say nothing. With Herod she always talked first, always gave herself away. She sat.

'I know you, Willa,' he said, 'I know you.'

Was he going to accuse her? It might relieve him. It might help.

'The way you'd do anything for anyone. The way you tip porters, not only that, but remember them, their mouths, something about them, you don't just re-recognize a porter by your own suitcase, you remember his face.'

He was not sarcastic. He was serious.

'Have a drink,' she said. He sat. She poured him a brandy. He took out a handkerchief and began to cry. She sat quietly. For something to do she rubbed her lids from time to time and at each rubbing a loose lash came out on her fingers and each time she stared at it as if by staring she might reach some solution to their predicament. Dry coughs escaped from her but she could think of nothing to say, nothing. After some time he stopped crying and put the handkerchief away. But he had the snuffles. He explained them away by saying that quicklime had got in his eyes, as if she hadn't seen his tears at all.

'Work is the only answer,' she said feebly. Next day she was going back to her glass like a woman going back to her children, excited at the prospect of re-seeing them, surprised that she had ever had the hardness of heart to leave. Glass delivered was still in crates with the 'Fragile' stick-on labels across the top. Each crate she would open, each sheet of glass lift out lovingly and with such care.

'Good God,' he said. 'You've no idea what I do, the man power, cuts, blisters, lacerations . . .' He held his hands out. 'The risks I have taken, moved cranes along the Great North Road, with jibs on, dismantled brine tanks, obnoxious gases, dismantled a cropping machine, blade nearly took the finger off me . . .' She squirmed.

'No witnesses,' he said.

'It's dangerous work,' she said.

'Ah I like danger,' he said and stood up, jutting his chin forward to meet it. She stood too. He touched her bottom pretending it was the feel of her suede skirt he wanted to experience.

'Rump that counts,' he said.

'Tom,' she said. He said it was the suede that had influenced him to act daft. The suede felt just like a little kitten. He said they should get a kitten.

'Sorry Willa,' he said then quickly.

'You came to see me,' Willa said.

'My pleasure,' he said, making a foolish attempt at a bow.

'This is business,' she said.

'Not altogether,' he said. 'I like to mix business with pleasure.' She offered him another drink even knowing it was a reckless move. He sat.

'I always knew we'd spend an evening like this, just the two of us,' he said.

'Don't be silly,' she said. 'It's a terrible time for all of us.'

'And not a friend.' he said. 'And not a friend.'

She ought to be cheering him up, she ought to be in control of things but she was not. What had they in common but what they'd both lost? Like two people who had warmed themselves at the same flame or inhaled a smell of the same rosebush. Where was Patsy at that moment? Safe in her man's arms, the coat over them, a child inside her, the man's arms, no morning sickness at least until morning. Willa thought of Auro and was certain that if he were there that night she could allow herself to be taken by him, so great was her need to be safe with a good man.

'What about it, Willa,' Tom said, 'a night out?'

'Some other time,' she said.

'No other time like the present. You know where they change the ashtrays after each flick. You remember telling us, how they do it, nicely, they put one over another, all ashtrays the same shape so that it's simple, like saucers, white saucers, they carry them away, covered, like they're carrying something nasty, that has to be hidden. Ashes!' And he laughed at the joke of it. He tipped his on the floor. Yes, she'd told them too much, she'd been too intimate.

'You said at the end of the night, leave the ashtrays, leave them until they're chuck full. Human touch!'

he said and licked his lips. Any minute now he'd say 'What's existentialism?' He was dead right. She'd put wrong ideas in their heads.

'I want a bit of fun,' he said.

'Well I don't know where you're going to get it,' she said frostily, but argued within herself that it was her duty to get him through. Her duty to him, her duty to Patsy, small repayment for the way they'd sheltered and cosseted her for over a year. She was on the rocking chair, her feet slightly raised to effect the back-and-forth jogging when she saw the toecap of his shoe stretch out to touch hers, she lost confidence and fell backwards. This of course enabled him to stand up and do the very thing she had tried to avoid – catch hold of her in a pretence at saving her.

'I think I must be very tired,' she said. Sometimes an admission of weariness or illness calmed even the very mad.

'I didn't sleep last night,' she said.

'You won't catch me losing a night's sleep,' he said and walked across to the corner cupboard where she kept the cigars for when she gave dinner parties.

'Take a cigar.'

'I don't.'

'Go on, it's a fine leaf . . . a great smoke.' He put one in her mouth so she accepted it.

'How do you like my lighter?' He flicked it on quickly, adroitly. It looked to be silver.

'It's lovely.' There would be a bank robbery reported in the morning.

She did not ask him to sit but he sat all the same, puffs of smoke circling over his head as he stretched and looked up, admiring the idle ascent of the smoke. She was letting hers go out.

'We're well away, peace without her.' He asked why

she hadn't gone long ago, why they hadn't tipped her out?

Willa sat on an uncomfortable chair, fearful, apologetic, making false starts in her head.

'You ought to get right away,' she said suddenly as if she was a lady sent by a travel bureau. To get him out of there was the important thing. And to think that there was a time when she cried out for contact with everyday life. She never learnt, never. Getting him out of there was the thing.

'Away! What for?'

'It can't go on you know, you here with me.'

'Oh I know that, I'm well aware of that factor,' but he made no move to go. She pretended to be falling asleep.

He smoked his cigar, asked for a little more brandy.

'What's this about sniffing it?'

Willa had given it to him in a wine glass and said it was not satisfying to sniff from that. He said how about a brandy glass then. She gave him one. In the snifter he rocked the brandy back and forth and rocked with it and said how luxurious life could be. She mentioned work and the word struck a false note in the room.

'Work,' he said, 'who wants to work? Take it from me, Willa, it's a mug's game, no one else goes straight, why should we? Any night clubs we'd like to go to, I have the good suit on, we go in there, on a par with any of them.'

'At this hour?'

'That's what you say to me, but what are you thinking, you're thinking undersized, aren't you?'

'There's no need to take offence,' she said, 'I thought we were good friends, always.'

'That's what I thought.' And he laughed, a hard, forced, frightening laugh. For a minute she thought that he was going berserk because it was not the laugh of a man making a joke.

'Don't fool around with me, don't ever fool around,' he said fiercely.

'But I'm not,' Willa said, 'I'm just sorry that it all turned out like this.' His desperation unknown and cumulative coming to a head.

'I appreciate that,' he said and he held the glass out and she rose and reluctantly put more in it. Because of her embarrassment and because of the strange way he looked she added more brandy than she had meant to. 'It's not that I want to be the victim any more,' she thought, 'it's just that I don't know how to handle any other role.'

'You know the one I'm sorry for,' he said and paused. He drank.

'You're the one I'm sorry for, Willa.' He repeated it. He was getting drunk, his words slurring into one another.

Exasperation was breaking loose inside her but she knew that it was important to appear calm.

'Tom,' she asked very soberly, 'are you leaving soon?'

'I wondered if I could have a bed for the night,' he said. 'All the hotels are closed now.'

'I suppose so,' she said. 'But you will have to go to sleep now.'

She put the brandy and the cigar-box in the cupboard and locked it. A thing she had never done before.

'Go on . . .' she said, and he rose and went out of the room without any unpleasantness. He was reeling a little.

*

She sat and watched the small boy sleeping peacefully in her brass bed. She tried to discern from his eyelids whether or not he was dreaming. She'd read an article about dreams and how it was possible to recognize the dreaming state in another by the way muscles twitched, but she forgot which muscles it was. Anyhow it was only a way of getting through. She thought of one thing after another but mainly of the absurd predicament of having no one but a small child to call upon for help. A predicament brought about by herself. She pushed friendship away, she pushed loves away, she built an artificial barrier, and like the dykes that kept the sea out of Holland it worked admirably. It was late when she sent Auro the telegram, ambiguously worded:

CAN YOU CONSIDER SLUICE GATES AGAIN?

The operator asked her to spell out sluice. She said,

'S for sin, L for loving, U for union, I for icicle, C for cochineal, E for enigma.'

The operator said she was very wide awake for that hour of the night. She said it was because she hadn't been to sleep. And when she put the phone down she laughed because she had made a joke, though unintentionally. Though a wan joke. If Auro came they would go away somewhere, away while Tom got out, and with the weight of real and drastic happenings going on around her the little phantom fears might assume their right place and dwindle into nothing, to be rubbed away with childhood's common-place transgressions. 'Middle of the night optimism,' she thought as she went back to sit in her bedroom.

*

Willa did not allow herself to hope that it would be Auro. More likely a team of demolishers, complete with implements, led by Tom. Still she answered the door, she had to. The person she had never expected to see again, in her life!

'Any room at the inn . . .?' Patsy said, battered, red in the face but not downcast. She said how she couldn't find him, how she'd been to the digs, how she'd been to the docks and nearly got herself impounded because he'd left without notice, and how she'd been six hours on a train. The way she said it made it seem that the train journey was the biggest inconvenience of all but she did that on purpose because she was determined now about keeping it to herself.

'We'll find him, we'll find him,' Willa said consolingly and brought her in.

In the kitchen Willa prepared tea. Patsy looked around, disgusted by its untidiness.

'Tell me what happened,' Willa said.

'Nothing to tell,' Patsy said. Talking about it took a bit more away each time and she wanted to keep the glory of him in her head. She needed that now. But like mercury it could run, it could slip out of her grasp. When talked about he got to be a shit and she didn't want that because he was no shit. All she wanted was to take off her coat and go back a year or go forward and feck all the talking, all the commiseration, all the spite. Tom in the pub telling barmaids, going from group to group with the tidings, like St John the Baptist; barmaids egging him on.

'I even went to the pub . . .' she said.

'What do you suppose happened?' Willa said, flat, discouraged.

'Afraid I suppose,' Patsy said, her voice neutral. No emotion, no criticism, no censure, no pity, no nothing. Inside herself Willa felt that she had learnt something good and thought how unfair that their lives had to be branded in order for her to learn. Once again she was being served by Patsy's adventure.

'It was my fault,' she said.

'Fuck whose fault it was,' Patsy said. What killed her was the way everyone thought of it as something that was over. Was. Was. Was. It would never be over now. They'd skimmed information, seen her letters, they tittered in Peckham but in the deep end they had not been able to see and they would never know how she loved him.

'What about Tom?' Willa asked. Patsy said she wasn't going back to him. She said it wasn't like using slot machines and going back to the first one if the second funked.

Willa showed the note he'd written saying he would leave on the next day. It was under the sugar bowl where he'd left it that morning.

It said that he was going, maybe to Ireland, maybe to the new world, it all depended on his frame of mind, but he expected he'd be no loss to anyone. Patsy read it but made no comment.

'There's a smell in this kitchen,' she said sniffing. Willa said that was what morning sickness did to a woman. Patsy said it was a corpse she was on about, not an unfortunate child. She located it. The potato that she'd stuck the pheasant's feathers in, less than a week before. She pitched it out. She said the place would go to rack and ruin without her. Willa said that was true. And without any reservation on either side they agreed that Patsy could come back as soon as Tom left. Willa said that for the time being Patsy would go to a hotel. Willa knew a nice hotel in the country, and it was a good time to be there to see leaves turning. She got a wad of notes from her bag and handed them to Patsy as they were, with a rubber band around them. Patsy looked out the window while taking the money. She was ashamed. The wall still half done. Ridiculous. All her hopes had sparkled, as white as the paint they'd applied to it. Ridiculous.

'And we'll finish that wall,' she said matter-of-factly.

'You'll have a rest in the hotel,' Willa said. It would be a grim rest, but still.

'Look,' Patsy said, 'if you took the coat back I wouldn't feel so bad.'

'There's no need to feel bad,' Willa said.

'I'd rather you did.'

'Are you sure?' Willa had already taken it back in her head. It was a beautiful coat as well as being Auro's only gift to her. A keepsake.

'I want you to,' Patsy said. The way she was now she wanted to be ugly and dowdy for a bit.

'All right,' Willa said, and she tried to hide the satisfaction she felt.

'How's your man?' Patsy said.

'Missing,' Willa said.

'You should take a bit of fun when it comes your way,' Patsy said softly. She knew about Willa's life, especially the torment of always sleeping alone.

'If it comes my way,' Willa said and they smiled at their manifold mischief as they climbed the stairs to pack Patsy's things. They put most of her belongings in boxes and hid these under Willa's bed. When Tom came in he would see the drawers emptied and he would be told by Willa that Patsy had come and cleared herself out completely.

'Wonderful,' Patsy said, 'the powers of contrivance!' and she tried not to picture his face when he came in and saw the room ravaged because a thing like that was much more definite than anything. She brought very few things with her, she wouldn't be needing them.

97

Willa hung the coat in her own wardrobe but said that they would own it jointly, and that they would wear it in turns.

For the second time in two days they parted.

'Never mind,' Patsy said, hearty all of a sudden, 'we'll have parties here, McBooing Booing singing ballads, hot turkey for all . . .'

'Christmas . . .' Willa said. Young turkeys were already in the shopwindows but she was not thinking of those, she was thinking ahead to when the baby was born, a pram in the hall, a gripe-water bottle on the kitchen sill, and she was looking forward to that.

Patsy moved. It was time to go. Something held her back. At last she blurted it out:

'You'll think it's funny but I wouldn't undo the past now,' she said, and they touched cheeks tenderly. At the gate Patsy turned round in the rain, raised her fist and shook it with friendly vehemence.

'Shoot your mother and father and build bridges,' she said. A joke about Germans, from one of their past moments.

The taxi-driver had the door open and he put the suitcase in the back along with her. He had his shoulders hunched up to keep the rain off his neck. While he was turning round they waved and Willa went on waving long after the car had gone out of earshot. Waving and crying. She was crying because life could be so beautiful, at times.

'Am I infringing on you?' Tom said as he sat by the kitchen table studying advertisements for flats.

'I'm going out,' she said, 'so I won't see you again.' Her way of saying it is the day for you to go.

'Oh I'll be gone, I'll be gone,' he said, with ominous woe in his voice. She said she'd send on his letters, to the job. They shook hands coldly.

'Mind if I use your phone?' he said.

'Use it,' she said tartly and went out.

There had been a tune playing in her head and she went out to buy the record. On the way she met people she knew and saluted them and spoke about the weather but she did not hear herself saluting or speaking because her mind was full of that tune and full of the obsession to get Tom out.

Alone in the gramophone booth she felt safe at last: white walls punctured with little circular holes and a stool to sit on, but she stood. Three songs preceded the one she hungered to hear. First a song about tears, then zoos, then pillows. The blonde woman who sang them had, according to the photograph on the sleeve, a squint in one eye. The songs were trashy but the woman made them work nicely because she put new twists into the feelings about zoos and tears and pillows. Willa thought maybe it was the squint that had impelled the woman to sing so.

'For those who fancy colouring books
    As certain people
    Here's a new . . .'

Willa had only to hear the first few words to know that she wanted it. A strange, freak happiness possessed her as she stood in the booth singing it in her head. She did not wait until the song had finished.

'I'll have it,' she said, rushing out to the counter. And she was happy all the time as the assistant took it off the player, put it in dull glass paper, then into its sleeve, sellotaped it, took the money and called on another assistant to witness the incoming five-pound note. Happy as she held it to her bosom and went down the street thinking how she would play it when she got in, put the kettle on, make tea, and with the mug of tea sit down and play it over and over again.

Tom was still there. He was writing on a pad.

'Well?' Willa said.

'Useless,' he said.

'What's useless?' she said. If only she'd stayed in that little white booth playing records all day, sitting when she wanted to, having lunch brought in on a tray, counting the punctures if things got bad, counting would be therapeutic like counting sheep at night. Also there were signals from the outside world – the word Pontiac and 'I was here dun,' and a Battersea telephone number with 'This Big' written after it. She would have been happy in that little booth, protected from all, no interference, nothing.

'All taken,' he said.

'Did you ring them?' she said. She wished she could strike him.

'All taken,' he said. He had written Paris, Patsy, Pants, Pansy on the pad and had also drawn the faces of flowers. If she were a man he would never take advantage of her like that.

'What are you going to do?' she said.

'That's what I'm debating,' he said. He had a booklet of Parks and Open Spaces and he unfolded it. Green blobs where each park was situated. He said Hampstead Heath looked best because it was biggest. Biggest blob of green on the white map where districts were written in red and the Thames a black snake coiled in and out between red lettering and various shapes of green.

'That might be one now,' she said, when the telephone rang.

'It isn't,' he said and he made no effort to answer it.

'Answer it,' she said hysterically. The telephone then stopped and its silence unnerved them just as seconds before its ringing had done. He was withdrawing his hand when it rang again and she jumped because she knew that it was for her.

'For you,' Tom said. 'Mr What's-his-name.'

She carried the telephone into the hall and he made no attempt to help her in getting the flex under the door.

'Is that you?' she said to Auro. Her heart somersaulting from so many different happenings.

'There's something I want to ask you,' she said.

'Something I want to ask you,' he said.

'What?'

'You ask yours first.'

'I want to go away with you for a night.'

'I want to go away with you.'

And each knew that the other was smiling then. She said where. He said leave it to him. They would go the next day. He said it would have to be by train as the car was needed. He didn't say 'Beryl needs it,' but Willa guessed as much and thought the first chink had come. They arranged to meet at a railway station and he said if it was the wrong one they would take a taxi to the right one. It was all simple and lovely now. She thrilled at the possibility of another chance. She felt relieved to escape from her house. She said he would see her a long way off because of the coat. He said he would see her anyhow because he was always on the lookout for her in crowds. He had never said anything quite so loving before.

The conversation quelled her anger. She said to Tom, 'I'm going away tomorrow, for a day, and be gone when I come back.' But said it like she was asking a favour. He gave her his word. He was trembling so badly that he took three matches to light a cigarette.

'Have something to eat,' she said.

'As a matter of fact it will suit me powerful, tomorrow is pay day and that was the obstacle, they want rent in advance.'

'Why didn't you tell me?' she said.

'I couldn't get across to you.'

And with a pang she looked away.

*

From the hotel Patsy wrote:

Dear Willa, I never had it so posh in my life. Breakfast in bed, my slippers laid out (the ones Tom gave me!!), the life of a lady. I wear my rings all day. It is a very select place, fitted carpets all over, fountains outside. The gardens are gorgeous, just like you said they would be. Of course I keep going back over everything. Tom came out the worst. Still it had to be. I know you read my letters, the dirty ones, but I don't want you to think I'm dirty right through. At times people feel like that – most people do. You are my only hope now. PATSY.

Patsy gave the porter a half-crown and dictated the address to him. He wrote in an old-fashioned hand. The way all old people write. He said it would go out in the afternoon post. She sat in her bedroom then and cried. She couldn't cry down in the lounge. When it got dark she walked to the end of the garden and looked at the sky. Not a soul around, the statues like ghosts. 'Ron,' she said, up to the sky, 'are you looking at the same star as me?'

Last night she dreamed so much. Nutty dreams. He and Tom both objecting to her hair style.

'Ron,' she said, looking up at the sky, 'it is thought that people dream for one and a quarter hours each night, well for one and a quarter hours I dreamed of you and then I wakened, what did I think of? You!'

Someone let out the dog. The dog came down, investigated, saw it was her, shuffled back. The dog had had a course in biting burglars. There were such places. The barman told her. They were money-mad. The owners. They even charged for billiards and the wireless in the room. Wicked.

'Ron,' she said, looking up at the sky, 'you didn't believe in me, why not?'

She knew now why rich women often threw their rings into the sea, or jumped from chandeliers, or lost their reason, because with idleness she was beginning to feel a bit like that herself. She couldn't enjoy anything, not even a feed.

She went past the fountains and up the steps, and the dog that had been trained to bite burglars slipped in along with her.

*

When Willa and Auro arrived the first thing that struck them was its unsuitability. It was a stone abbey with an annexe built on at a later date. The grounds very trim. High trees at the back, lower and lower ones sloping right down to a display of bushes that bordered the lawn.

A perfect gradient. The bushes on fire with berries, these berries too ribald, too much in that gentle calculated landscape. An elderly lady knelt before a rockery, trowelling.

'Not my scene,' Auro said, but they had let the taxi go.

On the doorstep two halves of a coconut shell that had been industriously pecked.

'What's that for?' he asked.

Willa said it must be for birds.

'Oh man . . .' he said, but grimly.

Inside the furniture had the radiance that only hard work can give it. Dismay held them nailed to the threshold. He rang the visitors' bell but hoped that there would be no answer. Willa hoped so too. A young girl appeared and conducted them up carpeted stairs and then up stone stairs to their room. The first thing Willa noticed was the four-poster bed, then the wash-stand, and the slop-bucket. It was cold.

'Can you bring us two large whiskies, with ice,' Auro said.

The girl said they had no licence.

'Oh God,' Willa thought, 'I'll never do it sober.' The curtains around the four-poster bed rattled fiend-ishly on the pole.

'Wait till I see Hagan,' Auro said when the girl had gone out. A friend of his, a fashion photographer, had booked the place for him.

'Never mind,' Willa said, partly out of embarrass-ment.

He sat on the bed to test the springs for sound. She began to unpack. Drawers came unstuck in the opening and she apologized at having to jerk them. Newspapers lined the drawers. She read the headings simply for distraction.

'Hey, it's a home for the aged,' he said. She raised

herself up on her knees and looked through the window. In the woods various couples were sauntering about. The leaves were russet, the couples elderly.

'I have no ring.'

'You can have mine,' and he threw it across to her.

Downstairs they pushed various doors open to find more or less identical scenes: a room with grand-father clock, more dark furniture, china ornaments, armchairs drawn up to the fire, boots drying inside fenders, people knitting, people dozing, women in networks forming the alliances they always form in convents, hospitals, asylums. The doors edged with horsehair opened noiselessly and as they looked into each room it was as if his blackness struck a spear among the networks of foregathered women. No one said anything. Even to Willa he seemed ten shades blacker.

'Wait till I get Hagan,' Auro said, out in the woods. They had put on raincoats and a lady in the hallway said 'Dressed for showers,' so that the silence barrier was down.

They were lovely woods, dense, jungly, disordered, old trees entwined, survived; some mad, covered in sick silverish moss. Autumn colours – brown, gold and pink to let the eye follow, but Willa was thinking of the bed-room, the four-poster, the rings rattling.

'I didn't know such places existed,' he said.

'In my childhood,' she said, 'there were slop-buckets and in the soapy water there were always burst cigarette ends.'

'All we need now is for Hagan to send one of his telegrams to be read over the phone – all-phallic-symbols-are-cock type of thing.'

'Oh God,' she said. It was like being back at school.

He said that probably they were vegetarian. He said to think that all over England there were places with a bar, billiards and T-bone steaks. He said again that he would kill Hagan but he was not angry about it.

'The roof of that bed looks as if it might cave in,' she said.

'Ah, love,' he said, 'we'll sleep on the floor,' and the blade of grass he had picked he whistled through until he got a little tune going. He knew all the latest tunes and spoke the words after he sang them. She told him about the record she'd bought the morning before. He said that was off the charts.

'If I fail you, you won't be cross?' she asked. Her deepest dread now that it might be lonelier after than before. Because with his going away there was no question of his being round to hound her with accusations.

'It is not a championship,' he said.

'Still it's important,' she said.

'Yes, it's quite important,' he said, and sighed. He looked at her.

'Who was that geezer you never told me about?'

'I'll tell you some time.'

'You went away to a hotel?'

'Yes, we were in a hotel.'

'And what did you do?'

'We hawed on cockroaches with our drunken breaths, and they came out of the cracks between the wood and stumbled up along the windows.'

'That was a fine thing to do . . . What else?'

'Don't ask me now, not now, not today.' They walked a bit in silence.

'Meanwhile back at the ranch,' he said, 'McBooing Booing and the Kerry Tiger have met and are locked in mortal combat straddled by Anna Livia Plurabella . . .'

'I should ring,' she said, 'and see if he's gone . . .'

'You shouldn't,' he said. 'It would only spoil our night.'

*

Tea was in the drawing-room. Trays laid for four were carried in by the proprietor and his wife. They welcomed Willa, and the husband – concealing his surprise badly – said 'Sir' to Auro. Guests stationed themselves around little tables, others stood taking pot luck. Auro was invited by the lady who had been trowelling to sit next to her. Willa followed. Seven hearing aids in sight. One lady with a travelling rug so that the lower half of her body was concealed. Had she legs? Willa looked down at the tea-tray – two scones per person, one bun iced, half a cherry in the centre, a choice of jams.

'I can't help thinking,' the lady troweller said, 'but that you're just married.'

'No we're not,' Auro said.

'Not just,' Willa said immediately.

'Not married,' the lady said and frowned. She told him her name. She was a Mrs Ormsby. She pointed out her husband. She said her Christian name was Mary but she was called Mary E since the time she was guest at a house party and there were two Mary's.

'How do you do – Mary E,' Auro said, and she liked that. She was flattered and didn't notice that he imitated her voice slightly. She asked what was he called. He told her. She said that was a pretty name and told it to her husband, spoke very clearly to her husband's hearing apparatus.

Those not wanting tea put a hand over their cups as the young girl went around bearing an exceptionally large enamel teapot. The proprietor's wife followed with coffee in a thermos. No chatter, only the sigh of the fire and gentle chewing. Auro an obscenity among

107

them. Too shiny, too young, too alive, too rapacious. His eyes could proposition any one of them, his lips wet the faces on which powder had been put but not dabbed on, he could unsettle the old bodies that smelt of pee, that smelt of powder, that smelt of lavender from handkerchiefs. He could make the men angry. Willa looked around, to measure the men's distaste. She smiled at one. He smiled back but through corneas silvered with age.

'Are you in a draught?' his wife asked him.

'There is a draught,' he said.

'Then sit elsewhere,' she said testily.

'I'm not sitting in it,' he said.

The telephone rang far away in the house.

'That's the telephone,' someone said, and then far away it was presumably picked up and answered and they waited in silence – Willa in dread – as if fatal news was going to be delivered, then when it wasn't a little conversation started up.

'It must be very hot in Africa just now,' the lady with the rug around her said to Auro. The entire room seemed to wait on his reply and through it to pass verdict on him.

'Man from Aldgate, that's me,' he said and smiled. 'But my father was a Jamaican.'

Now she was embarrassed and she said in a shrill voice to the room at large, 'I was sent a postcard from Durban that I never received.'

'You should have reported it,' someone else said and they fell to talking about the inefficiency of all those who were employed in a public capacity. Auro and Willa were the first to escape.

'Did you like your tea?' Willa said.

'I tasted a bun which was vile.'

'They're in love with you – the ladies.'

'Ah, they know where the old golden bouillon is.'

'Ssh . . .' she said.

But she knew that a few days in his company and she would be in love with him, badly.

*

Tom sat back in the sofa and clapped. He was clapping himself. The needle slithered over the record and he heard:

> 'For those who fancy colouring books
> As certain people do . . .'

but got up to change it because that was not the song he felt like hearing.

First there was harsh guitar strumming and then:

> 'Close the door, light the light
> We're staying home tonight . . .'

'Precisely,' he said. He talked back to the song. About how he'd beaten them all. Beaten them at their own game. Lies. Cunning. Deception. They took him for a mug. Willa with the cock-and-bull story about Australia and how Patsy left no forwarding address. Unseemly hints about the notice in the post-office: 'Australia for your children's future.'

'I've got nothing against kids,' he said. Willa the phoney, on about destiny and the hidden currents of the heart. Too sensitive to bid him goodbye. Left a note – 'Would you be so kind as to leave the key, there is a tin of salmon for your supper. Goodbye!' And he had only to go upstairs to root around for a suitcase to find their whole plot exposed – her clothes, her alarm clock, the coffee set his aunt gave them. The way they'd ratted on him. Then the letter. 'Tom came out the worst!' Not but that the letter was his biggest ally. After he found the suitcase he stopped at nothing. He ransacked every place. Opened all letters – letters about narrow-fitting shoes and agriculture in China. 'Tom came out the worst!' Oh no, boy, Tom didn't.

> 'Oh my love
> Oh my love
> I cried for you so much
> Lonely nights without sleeping
> While I longed for your touch.'

'Love,' he said furiously. He hated her now. Should have hated her long ago, old scum-flecked lips, crooked, brought him to the bottom of his misery. Marvellous the way he got over loving her. A miracle. No pain whatsoever. Couldn't wait to do it. He put it around his own neck like a collar and practised in the mirror. They'd had a recitation at school:

> 'Malachy wore the collar of gold
> Which he won from the proud invader.'

A useful little weapon and no licence necessary. Of course not everyone had the technique. Tight, tighter and tightest. Plenty of experience with chickens. Saturday-morning routine long ago, his mother saying 'Kill a chicken, go to confession.' His poor mother, reared six of them, never complained, if she got a toffee she cut it in six, women were not like that any more.

The telephone rang and he put the wire in his pocket quickly. He went into the kitchen. It could be her or it could be Willa ringing to see if he'd checked out. He smiled when it stopped. Kept his hand in his pocket and got a nerve-snapping thrill when he felt it. Telephone shot his nerves but apart from that he was all right. He looked at his hands, they'd see him safely through.

Stubby but useful. Prying things open, prying things shut, there was nothing they couldn't do to her. It would be quick and it would be clean. Not that she deserved a clean death, not that she deserved a clean death.

He rang his friend Counihan.

'Is that you, Counihan?

'This is Tom speaking.

'Oh powerful, powerful altogether . . . I've a blonde in.

'Look I won't be in tomorrow, see that everything is all right will you, cover up . . . Yes, she's in the room. 'Bye.'

Counihan said he would cover up and made a sucking noise at the other end of the telephone when he heard the bit about the blonde, but didn't believe it. Counihan had an arm missing and trusted no one. Sensible man.

Then he sent the telegram – he sent it to Mrs Tom Wiley although he begrudged letting her use his name.

COME HOME TOMORROW NOT BEFORE SEVEN. HE WILL BE GONE. NO NEED TO RING. ALL SAFE. LOVE. WILLA

And then he laughed at his strategy. It would be dark. He'd wear her gloves. That hedge was poor camouflage but it would be dark. She'd have a suitcase, impede her moves. He'd go out there around six. Make himself comfortable. Bring cough drops in case of a tickle in the throat. A scarf to put over his face. Then Ireland. His mother would stand by him. That's what your mother was for. All her genius hiding blokes during the time of the Black and Tans would come in useful. His mother kept a man for a week in a pit of potatoes. She could get that pit open.

He made tea and had it with biscuits. Biscuits were

a great consolation. There was only one important thing and that was to get a good night's sleep. Sleep was vital to keep the nerves oiled. Good ad for the telly that! Each time he put his hand in his pocket he felt the nerve-snapping thrill, through it his mess was going to be solved, through it he'd be the man she never took him to be.

'Where are you, where are you?' he said. The record had stopped and he'd missed most of it while phoning. He went back to the sitting-room and put it on.

*

They were sitting in the hall next to a supply of very dark umbrellas when Willa decided she would like a smoke. They crossed the lawn, taking quick steps, for fear of being followed. The turf was wet. In the kitchen garden they stood, quite a distance away from the lights of the house, and when he struck the match he looked at her, first.

'I never took a picture of you,' he said. 'Why is that?'

'I mustn't be pretty,' she said.

'That's what you say,' he said and lit the cigarette. The smell of sulphur first and then the whiff of cigarette, as the smoke distributed itself through the darkness, and the night air fresh and nippy and the smell of earth combined with the smell of cigarette and the two of them in the most secret moment they had had, guilty of misdemeanour, waiting for a gong to go.

'The dinner will be scrumptious ... they're not vegetarian,' she said.

'The dinner will be vile,' he said and delivered up samples of the conversation they might expect: 'Ernestine is expecting a baby in January ... do you like pudding ... military connexions ... difficult getting to Hampstead by bus ...' and then he stopped. 'Ah, what do we care,' he said and ran his finger along her neck and throat, saying it was like a white column in the dark. She had put on pendant ear-rings and a black satin dress with wide georgette sleeves. She said that her neck, the thin ear-ring chains that tapered to an oval stone, the dress with sacramental sleeves were things donned in an attempt to escape her true self and assume another self.

'You see before you another me.'

'Each and every love is terrible,' he said, sweeter sounding than a thousand daydreams, and then as if to drench her in sweetness he said, 'I don't think I'd spend a night here with anybody else.'

At dinner they were put sitting opposite. Mrs Ormsby said that husbands and wives were separated at table because it gave both parties something to look forward to. Willa sat next to a man who said he lived in the Winston Churchill electorate area but that of course Sir Winston Churchill was dead. A tureen of soup was brought in; its steam running ahead down the length of the table reminding Auro of the warm place he should have brought her to. He would do everything for her. She had something lovely, china had it, girls he didn't know, some that he did know, a timidity.

The maid brought brown rolls that were shaped like small loaves.

'Oh very swagger,' Miss Craven said, selecting one. 'Must be in honour of the young people.' She sat at the head of the table and had first of everything. She asked if there was marrow with dinner and when the maid said yes a little cry of satisfaction went up as if marrow denoted some sort of victory.

'Not that we can excuse those potatoes you gave us at lunch,' a woman farther down said.

They spoke in low voices. Each sentence solitary,

frozen, delivered to the room at large. They ate, they spoke, they ate, spoons dropped on the rims of soup plates, then came a lull. Hands lay on the table, half curled, ready to contract, hands were brought to mouths to shut in a burp, hands fiddled nervously with cruets and the shy creature on Willa's left was lost in a reverie that induced her to keep offering crusts to an imaginary animal under the table. The dishes of vegetables were passed down one side, the platter of carved meat down the other. The man next to Willa skewered three pieces on to his fork with one lunge.

'What do they say – that salt gives you a head-cold,' he said to Willa, not looking up to see the disapproval meant for him. He poured the gravy very sparingly.

'I haven't heard that,' she said. She was certain that she had started to menstruate.

'I saw you down by the doves,' the shy creature said as she leaned across to get Auro's attention. Mrs Ormsby had monopolized him completely and among the women there was pique.

'Oh yeh . . .' Auro said. Willa thought he was going to laugh.

'I'll say you enjoyed that cigarette . . .' Not so absent after all. Then she turned in case Willa might be hurt and said, 'I wish I had your skin.'

'You have a good skin,' Willa said.

'Had . . .' she said. They did not know what it meant to have been beautiful, to have had winter vacations in sunny places, to have picked shells on beaches and fall in love with the first stranger one met. Her eyes misted over because her thoughts were suddenly too painful and she got up and hurried out, her little cloth purse bouncy against the flowers of her long dress.

'Poor Betty,' one of the men said.

114

Willa wished she could do the same. She wanted to know for sure. In a way it might solve everything. After dinner she would hurry away to see.

'I think you're a bohemian,' Mrs Ormsby was saying to Auro, her face lifted to his, the nose heavily sprinkled with powder, the powder not rubbed in. Her husband, a little way down, looked rapt, admiring, and said to Willa, 'If you buy a canary you've got to let it sing.'

But Willa was thinking of her own house, deserted, waiting, in darkness, waiting for someone to come home to it, nothing but the two blue pilot lights in the gas cooker showing signs of life. Tom gone. She rang and there had been no answer. Left behind were the beer barrels he'd painted and filled with flowers, the clipped hedge, the rooms painted in light colours, the ceilings done in blue, his labours outlasting his life in that house. Poor Tom.

'There is a way of tackling hiccoughs,' the man next to her said as he demonstrated on a tumbler of water. The trick was to drink but in drinking to stretch the upper lip so that it reached the rim of the glass. But in demonstrating he managed to give himself hiccoughs and this sent a wave of laughter around the table. Those who had been quiet or eating greedily looked up from their plates and began to laugh though they did not know why and once they started they forgot to stop. He tried holding his breath but each time another hiccough escaped and each time the laughter grew louder. The maid coming in with the pudding was surprised by such gaiety and said aloud that she had forgotten the custard and this like a meteoric joke passed across the family atmosphere and the men said to each other, 'She has forgotten the custard.' The slightest incongruity seemed to be the beginning of still another round of laughing. People talked without bothering to finish their sentences. They were remembering other funny things that had happened around that table, because although some were on a visit, some like Miss Craven had been there for years. Their thoughts were suddenly brimming and they remembered naïve incidents from the past as when a frog came out of the fire, or the coffee jugs were filled with hot water only, or a pebble was found in the lentil soup. And these they told to Auro. Mrs Ormsby asked him what he did for recreation. She asked if he would have a little game with her after supper. He looked at Willa, 'Backgammon,' Mrs Ormsby said.

'No whist . . .'

'No stunts . . .'

'Yes, stunts . . .' two or three women said and clapped, but the man with the hiccoughs said it had better be 'Blind man's Buff' because that didn't exclude anyone. They ran from the dining-room and even those who normally stayed to stack the dishes ran too because they did not want to miss any of the fun.

Willa took the opportunity to go upstairs and see. She locked the door, then put on the light and was grievously disappointed to find that her fears were unfounded. From her cosmetic bag she got the magnifying mirror in an attempt to examine herself. She studied her face, her face was no surprise to her, big and jowly in that mirror, her breasts enormous so that she had to look at them with the naked eye to make sure they had not swollen, her belly white, a white dune over which sun or love never travelled, and then down, down to the seat of her fear – she opened her legs, her stomach felt hollow, it was as if it was being cut out of her, or wrenched out of her, her whole being was being sundered apart. She couldn't go on. She put the mirror away, sat on the bed doubled up, cradling her body with her arms. 'It's a coffin I need,' she thought, and she put on some scent and dipped her fingers in the water jug before going down.

*

Downstairs the game was in full swing. Auro's spotted handkerchief was around a lady's eyes. He had his jacket off and he winked at Willa as she came in. The lady stumbled about in spirals saying 'What a lot of you,' and Auro stood still so that she could catch him. When he was blindfolded he moved about quickly threatening them with childish squeals, and they bumped and dodged and shrieked with laughter. Mostly the women shrieked but the men liked it too. He moved as though swimming, his arms weaving in and out – missing them just a little. He made it exciting for them. Sometimes he stood still and snapped his fingers as if he was plotting some new method. And then he set to again and the shriekings started up. He rolled up his sleeves. The polish on his arms like that on the furniture. Willa got behind a curtain because she did not want it to be her, but in fact it was. He let go at once. 'Not you,' he said, moving in another direction. Betty was at the other end. He got her by the chain of her purse and she slid closer to him like a woman gliding into a waltz and already lost in the melody of it. He touched her long nose, her high brow, her flickering cheeks where she had applied rouge since dinner-time. She smiled with a dazed expression.

'It would be Betty,' a woman's voice said from the far end.

'Betty,' Auro said. Some clapped. He pulled the scarf down on to his neck and she stayed within his arms.

'Would you like to see my trinkets?' She unclasped the purse and took out some of her possessions – a red leather wallet so cracked that the cracks were like a design upon it, a silver pill box, two lumps of sugar in case she met a horse, and a piece of string. Then having shown them she seemed a little sorry as the very private are the moment after they have revealed themselves, and she drifted away pensive. Willa watched. 'Each cries alone,' she thought. These women who smelt of pee, who smelt of powder, who smelt of lavender from handkerchiefs the stencils of her future self. 'I must not end my days like that,' she thought, paying no attention to the game.

Some got out of breath, some listened to the chime of the clock, checked with their own watches and said 'A quarter after.' Husbands warned wives 'Mustn't overdo it,' wives said peevishly 'I'll find my own way thank you,' there were momentary huffs and various cries of dismay as the trolley of hot-water bottles was wheeled in, labels affixed to each one. Some took one, some took more than one. Auro and Willa were last to go. They stood with their backs to the fire, warming themselves, talking about the different people. He recognized those who wanted to start life all over again, because they put the most enthusiasm into the game. And Willa said she had never learnt games but that she must start. In their bedroom the smell of perfume was excessive. She had forgotten to put the glass stopper on the bottle.

*

'Hear that,' he said, 'and that.' A wind, the curtain rings, an owl, whatever the sounds she did not fear them. Nor the shadows ambling across the floor. Having only one bed simplified her decision. They did not get involved with discussions because for that night there was no choice and she could not send him away.

'The first time is never the best,' he said, not boasting.

He was talking, traversing her, finding the ins and

outs of her, unflicking sorrowful, joyful, glorious mysteries and she was admitting and consenting and stretching and crying, her resistance as ferocious as her hunger and he saying p for pity and d for damp and l for loving and f for fucking and p for pity as she begged yes and no in an impossible ravelled voice.

'No, no, no,' she said closing up but too late, closing him in, securing what her voice said it wanted to keep out and his teeth biting the hair of her underarm as his thumb parted the hair of her underneath, and his hands fingering and delecting and hurting and the thumb keeping the vent open and his voice saying softly 'pity, pity, pity,' and his fingers going faster and faster and her head and neck and arms tossing back and forth vehemently with animal tosses and he smiling through it all not at his expertise but at her unimpeachable deceit at the resisting head, neck and voice, all devoted to the utterance of no, and her limbs begging no, and all of her being saying no except for one soft little central screech of skin and this saying yes louder and stronger and fiercer than all the other orchestra of nos and his fingers giving the totality of their love, their touch, their strength, their heat, their hostility, their stretch, their fury, their patience, their cruelty, their softness, their nimbleness, their kneading and their love to that most secret and central cause in her. And her voice was intermittent as her panting increased and finally when his body covered hers the panting replaced the words they might have said.

They lay locked until the last shudders died down in them and sounds of the outer world – the wind, the owl, the curtain rings – were heard again.

'I was on an aeroplane once,' he said, 'and they undercharged me by one hundred and fifty dollars.'

She dropped off to sleep hearing him say that, promising that she would waken in a little while and make love to him as he had done to her. And she did.

In the morning he moved quietly as though he had no strength. She opened her eyes, steeling them against the light. She smiled at him.

'I should like to stay asleep,' she said, and finished the sentence in her mind, 'before again finding that I am alone.'

'You keep your mouth closed when you're asleep,' he said.

'Is that wrong?'

'You should open it to let the poison out.'

'I'll remember that,' she said. Her hands in the fleece of his hair.

'In the snow . . .' she said idly.

'In the snow . . .?' he asked idly.

'Your eyelashes would become white . . .' His lashes were a different texture to the fleece of his hair. They were extra long and beautifully parted as if they had been carefully oiled and the parting then done mathematically.

'Soldier's wife,' he said, 'I'll be home for Christmas.'

'Do you look better or worse on no sleep?'

'They put out forest fires by creating a vacuum.'

'What does that mean?'

'Abstinence . . .' he said. She did not care. She felt warm, at peace, oddly wise. He could go. She would live on her pliant dream, she had lived on less. She would weigh him against Herod hour by hour, day by day. In her mind she saw a tiny letter scale with brass pans and little delicate brass weights that had to be caught by tongs and in her mind one of the pans was tipping violently as if there were no question of things being in the balance. Down the Herod road she need not go. She lay with the soles of her feet exposed airing them, not frightened that they might be touched, because of course they had been.

*

In the long, bare dining-room the people were the strangers they had been at the very beginning. The incident of the night before hardly left any traces. Very few seemed to remember. Willa did not care. She was sitting at table drinking tea, it was harvest time, someone's boiled egg was left uncracked and hairpins were falling in showers over a white bread-plate. Or was it one hairpin that her fancy multiplied into a shower. She was thinking of Auro. He sat opposite. To be thinking of him while he sat opposite a crowning pleasure. She moved her weight from one buttock to the other. An ache going through her, and after-pleasure, in the crevices he had been, in the high and the low of her a sweet discomfort and the glorious testament – 'Kilroy was here'. She laughed and he caught her laughing and shook his head at such frivolousness.

*

Out in the woods he gathered her as if a sheaf. The sheaf for that harvest. The russets of the trees like wine starting to ferment. The russets of their love like that too. Not a bitter love at all, not a melancholy walk.

'In a way I'm glad you're going,' she said. He knew what she meant.

'It will stretch it,' she said.

'Stretch it . . .' he said, and they stood apart and like children stretched until the tips of their fingers met. He did other childish things – he shinned up a tree, he squelched puff-balls, he shadow-boxed with a pool of rain.

In the train they scarcely talked. Her body marked by his teeth was hidden away under that luxuriant coat. A year ago he loved Beryl, thought he had come to the end of his wanderings, but it was not so. He was on another cliff. Glad about it, sorry about it. Sorry for Beryl. They'd go to Canada, they'd be together for a bit yet but it was on the wane. No one's fault. A man went from one to the other, flotsam and jetsam, the sum of girls adding up to the definite One. Women were different: women were like the mistletoe, they had to live off a man's strength.

'I want to take you with me,' he said.

'You can't.'

'But I still want to.' And she shook her head back and forth, pressing it on the linen that protected the headrest.

'What age are you?' She needed to know something substantial about him, some small fact to set alongside the dream and the speculation.

'At school,' he told her, 'we were taught the exports of countries by diagram, 80 per cent cocoa, 75 per cent tar oil, 50 per cent leather, $2\frac{1}{2}$ per cent iron ... the diagram like a New York skyscraper, various peaks, various ages.'

'What are you youngest at?'

'Loving ...'

'Oldest at ...'

'Fucking I suppose ...'

She took both his hands, held them, then kissed them. She would never be able to mistrust him, she would never be able to give him Christ-like standards for which she could upbraid him when he failed.

'Do what you must do,' she said. For that moment at least, she meant it. And a moment was something. It would return of course, the other thing, the base, unlovely dependence, the bleakness, the loneliness, the pointless purgatory that was her wont, but for the moment she was as he said – happy and saturate with not a bother on her.

'You say very composite things,' she said, repeating it for him.

'I'll have to watch it,' he said, 'I mistrust all-in statements.'

'So do I,' she said. She slipped off the ring that he had loaned her.

They would say goodbye, they would not strike bargains, they would let time and the seasons and their two natures decide the future. They were not even sad at parting.

At the station he watched her go down on the escalator – not a single taxi – and he watched while the figure descended into the pit of the Underground, and then he went automatically to telephone Beryl to say he was home.

*

Willa walked from the station. There was a light drizzle, at once soothing and refreshing. She let it lick her face and eyes, those eyes tired from interrupted sleep. He was going away and it was a pity, maybe it was just as good. It couldn't last – what man loves a tormented woman for long, what man is fool enough? She walked quickly as if expecting to find him at home ahead of her, she half hoped, but knew the covetousness of that hope and still she walked quickly. At times she slung the carrier bag over her shoulder and through the canvas a spike (the edge of a book) kept prodding her back, but discomfort was no matter. She cheered at the thought of rooms warmed by the mere turning of a knob, made boisterous by the turning of another, happiness once she started to cook: she would make toast, restart a service-able life, unpack the crates of glass, and bevel out her tribute to him and to life with this frangible substance. The loss of him would not set in for days and even when it did it would be good loss with a sweet reverberation. She walked without any nervousness. On dark nights in the city of London women were raped but she was not going to think about that. She looked at the sky – a field of stars. She looked down the street – they'd mended the light, sodium blue lights at regular intervals sucking the life mercilessly from the road's gleamed surface. Somewhere on the other side of the equator a field of daisies. Above all she had no fear of him. Some-thing had been accomplished. She felt that she could even confront Herod, point out to him that at bottom, like her, he was deeply afraid; and those she liked she liked with a little more patience, a little more love, she would telephone those friends that she had neglected because of work and the week's commotion, no, she would write, letters were less obligating and she would offer some of the nicer bonds of friendship – a drink, food, flowers, a joke. It turned out not to be possible because Tom who had been waiting since six o'clock for the appearance of the coat rose as she went through the gate and acted so deftly that the scream she let out got lost in her throat as a wail. She died with her back to him and as she fell he helped her down.

It was Tom's own unceasing howl that called the alarm. 'God strike me dead,' he said when he saw the mistake he had made, and he kept saying it. A boy learning to ride a bicycle called his mother and one by one the neighbours came out of their houses, and gathered round, those who for years had been steadily minding their own business, those who were callous strangers to her as she had been callous stranger to them.

There was a small obituary in which it was claimed that the loss to a declining art was considerable. Auro changed his flight to be present for the funeral and afterwards Patsy gave him the bundle of letters written to him. He wished she hadn't, not only because they were a new burden but because they were a new Willa and he was sufficiently heartbroken over the loss of the old one not to want to know the darkest side. But he read:

Dear Auro,

Herod said he felt he had been sent to save me from falling over a cliff. He also said honey produces sweet breath. You find yourself well disposed towards a man like that.

Dear Auro,

Herod supplied the cliff. There were pleasure walks and constitutional walks and cliff walks on Sunday. The high cliff behind his house. (Indeed as time went on his house dissolved a little back into the cliff itself.) You would put your hand out to balance yourself and get sheared not by thorns but through thorn, through moss, through scrub by the red stone's edge. He would set a destination each time, a point to which I must scramble. I said I would do anything else, dust the piano, make bread, saw wood, but he said 'You will do this.' Sometimes I didn't care. I would put my foot into a little opening in a rock – brought about by a trickle of water – and think that the rock above might have pity on me and bury me, but it didn't. Once I relied on a piece of grass to save me, asked too much of one blade of grass. But he caught me. Always when I fell Herod caught me. He caught me with such expertise as if we were on stage and it was a fall we had rehearsed over and over again. 'You see you need me to save you from . . .' – how he said it!

Dear Auro,
It was in a remote part of Switzerland, not far from the German border. An abandoned sanatorium, obliterate flowerbeds, vine-leaves yellow with disease and no wonder because the place had not been inhabited for years. The grass to his chalet needed scything. Even when trampled on with our boots it never lay flat, was always making up its mind to rise again. The house was on two floors and we had separate rooms.

Dear Auro,
He had had a mother and a father and a sister. They had lived in a walled town with a castle, outside mountains, lakes. In the winter they went on sleighs and ate kohlrabi. A fairy tale.

Dear Auro,
'It won't be easy, it is not going to be easy, but I think you are going to enjoy the struggle.' He said many plants need a period of severe cold in order to encourage germination. 'In England,' he said, 'dull old England, Himalayan primroses appeared after the harsh winter of 1962–3.' Not that I wanted to be a primrose!
And yet we were near. Too near for happiness.

Dear Auro,
I asked to be brought out to rejoin the world. We passed a coffin, or rather a coffin passed us, where we had stopped, outside an inn. The hearse was speeding and there were no flowers. Still I blessed myself. We tried pushing the wooden door of the inn, but it did not yield. I pounded the iron knocker but to no avail. The inn was closed. The season was

over. I said weren't there other inns. He said if the season was over in one place it was over in another. I was disappointed. I had pinned a lot of hope to that outing. We drove to the village. The only gay thing was a patch quilt flapping on a clothes-line. We shopped. He spoke German. He was understood perfectly by the shopkeeper.

Dear Auro,

Evenings were best. There were fewer crises, fewer breaches, lamplight, a sort of peace. I wore a clean shirt and tied my hair back with a ribbon. Sometimes he said complimentary things. He said, 'I would like very much to have you for a friend.' He said, 'I don't know what is coming over you, Willa McCord, but you are getting better and better.' He said, 'Your eating gives you away.' I began to cry. He skimmed them off with his finger, the way you skim cream. He said, 'What a lot of tears you need. And what a lot of punishment.'

Dear Auro,

A back issue of *The Times* came wrapped around some English tea. He opened it and read: 'Even distinguished surgeons have been known to make a mess of topping their breakfast egg. Scalpels, tweezers and swabs are of no avail. The answer is, or rather was, the neat little toppers our grandfathers used. Shaped like scissors but ending in a ring (which held the egg) and a circular blade, they decapitated without fracture or haemorrhage.' I put my hands to my ears, said no but he said once information has gone in it makes its own inevitable way along the spiral cavity of the internal ear. He said what about the hairpins I poked the ear with. What about that. When I calmed down he kissed the crown of my head. A sweet dry brother's kiss. He said, 'Poor poor Willa engulfed within yourself!' I cherished that. I do believe he was a hypnotist.

Dear Auro,

When he gave me flowers – phlox in fact – he had

bandaged wet rag around the stems so they would stay fresh for a long time, and that, I loved. By means of a sundial he taught me to know the true noon when the shadow is briefest, not the noon of crazy clocks. And that I also loved. I always walked a little behind – like a dog – following the meander of his thoughts.

Dear Auro,

First my return ticket cashed to buy bread. Then my passport that I kept in a drawer between the folds of a turquoise slip. No longer there. He said it was safe, with his. Lastly my private parts. Their structure and their dread known only to Herod, and to Herod's finger at that. It was day when he drew the shutters and carried me down the ladder stairway to his own quarters. Pitch dark there also. Not a crack of light. We lay on a plank bed. He remained fully clothed. Sometimes it was my finger, sometimes his that he put in both our mouths and wound round both our tongues to put in my second secret mouth to stir up fears and funny-nerves and then as I began to rise and fall and want for it he took all fingers away, mine and his and locked them in his clench while I begged wildly with mouth and words and cursing supplication and he said no no no and rising and falling to nothing I got carried away on a little solitary flood hearing nothing but the echo of his laughter. It did not take long – seconds. He said how unmelodious the cries of satisfied desire are, an extraordinary fact but true. I said I was sorry. He said how glad he was that he had given me the special opportunity to be myself. I said nothing to that. Against the wall – my eyes had got trained to the darkness – there was the bulky outline of the mattress. I said 'Is that the mattress?' He said 'Of course, you wouldn't want it to be comfortable would you?' I put out my hand. The walls were granular to the touch.

Dear Auro,
    . . . fragment and riddle and dreadful chance.

128

Dear Auro,

I dreamed. A hare on its hind legs, as high as my face, licking it clean. An excess of saliva on the hare's tongue, the tongue itself ridged like a ploughed field, and tough. Tough as leather. I came awake trying to wipe the spittle off and shoo the hare away.

Dear Auro,

He said, 'Once upon a time I was coming home along the street with a bag of oranges when I was overtaken by a friend. He was on a bicycle. He asked for some. I said no. They were for the family. Then before I could thwart him he took the bag and cycled off at an unimaginable speed. When he was some distance ahead he began to drop the oranges one by one along the road and of course they rolled into the gutter and were rendered useless.'

It was my turn:

'Once upon a time I was out for a walk and I began to menstruate. I didn't know what it was because no one had told me and still I did know because I was not surprised. I was frightened. I couldn't walk. I could neither go back nor go forwards. I forget how I got home.'

'I knew you then,' he said, 'I am the only person who has ever known you.'

'I was going to say I was assaulted but it wouldn't have been true.'

'It would, it would, we invent less in lies and in dreams than in actual confession.'

(How right that is. How right that is.)

We were united. And oh I have to say it, I loved him – a foolish love, a stupid love, but true. We sat very close together crying, for ourselves, for each other, for the small catastrophes that yield great consequence. Our griefs matching like two odd gloves, two odd gloves from opposite ends of Europe, our guilts matching like that too.

Dear Auro,

But there was no going back to the world. He said it was

too late, it was already too late when I came. 'Oh other world,' I used to think, 'why are you not sending search parties out?' Things from my pre-life though not particularly thrilling at the time assumed a sweet and disproportionate importance. I remembered seeing one evening at dusk, a large bunch of white flowers on the back seat of a taxi and I thought of the joy they brought, arriving, according to my reckoning, at nightfall, unaccompanied, with a little card testifying to friendship, maybe to love. 'Oh other world,' I thought, 'why should you send search parties out – I washed my hands of you too remorselessly and too soon.'

Dear Auro,

November the month of the suffering souls. The conifers around the house were crying. The trees the hired mourners of our fate. I said, for something to say, 'The trees are crying.' He said, 'Trees don't cry, they weep.' I thought, 'He is not talking about trees, he is talking about us.' 'Are you talking about us Herod?' 'That is your trouble,' he said, 'you do not think historically.' Throttled.

Dear Auro,

The marriage ceremony was grim. It was held in a Roman Catholic church, because he said the old mythology dies hard in all of us. It was in the sacristy, and the witnesses were strangers. There was a dispute afterwards about money, and I smelt something rancid, which must have been the wax of the altar candles.

Dear Auro,

And I prayed, I prayed for appendicitis to be able to get out of there.

Dear Auro,

> Jack Spratt could eat no fat,
> His wife could eat no lean,
> And so between them both you see
> They licked the platter clean.

All perfectly agreeable until Mrs Jack Spratt's digestion altered, which is why people have to change at exactly the same ratio, otherwise the balance is destroyed. In my mind I wanted to go but the rest of me did not chime in.

Dear Auro,

His uncle – a fiddler – sawed his right hand off rather than serve with the Germans. If his uncle was anything like Herod I bet he often held the fiddle close to his craw and with his withered wrist sawed bitter noiseless tunes. It is no use making a great gesture unless you intend to live by it, which is why death is the easiest sacrifice. Hurrah for martyrs. In love with Herod and death at the same instant.

Dear Auro,

You ask why I ever went. Not unreasonable. I went for a holiday. He had gone back there anyhow. He said the mountains and the fresh air were awfully invigorating. A thoughtful man of thirty-eight, his malady a well-kept secret. I was glad to get away from the coffee shop and the noise. When I first arrived he gave me the plant and animal lore, respected my privacy, soon had me in his grip, like a flower in the grip of leaf at night. I wrote a letter to my boss saying among other things, 'I will be home next week,' but Herod erased it with a piece of fresh dough. (He made bread. Each loaf had the design of a cross.) By the time he unearthed my flaw it was too late to go; another grip altogether. 'Judge to what degree I love you,' he said as he drew the bolt of the door, and like a fool I smiled, thankfully.

Dear Auro,

He said 'You wouldn't survive a day in the world. You live in confusion and shame.' He said I ought to be thankful that he had volunteered to be my keeper. There were cow-bells and sheep-bells but I had stopped hearing them.

Dear Auro,

Constitutional walks and cliff walks and pleasure walks. A circular bough across a gorge. He stepped on, his body vacillating, then he caught my hand and brought me on with him. It was a circular bough about twelve inches in diameter. I kept losing my grip because the wood was wet. I don't know how I made it. But I have to say that at the other side there was such a moment between us when he held his arms out and I clung to him in an aching passion, everything spilled over, such a spill of love, of passion, of achievement. And I saw myself swept and helpless in the torrent and I knew that it was as he said – 'You do not go because you would rather have a man that punished you than one who did not, because you are a woman.'

Dear Auro,

He was trepanned but too young to have been fighting in the last war. (He was thirty-eight.) Trepanned in peace time I expect. He had uncles in new blocks of flats in Cologne – transplanted uncles from another country. I said what about his mother, his father, his sister, the kohlrabi, the rides on sleighs? But these things, so inherent to his original fairy tale, dropped out of the story. 'You didn't believe that twaddle did you?' he said, and laughed at how gullible I had been.

Dear Auro,

We had a beautiful evening. Cancelling out all the whittling, all the grief. In a hotel. No one but us. Round tables, long wine glasses with green stems, three chandeliers hanging low from the ceiling and reflected in the bow of the window, so that in the garden they went on for ever towards the mountains. We drank strong wine and ate pickled herrings while we watched them lay the table. There was cake. It had already been cut but impossible to tell that because the knife mark had sunk into the deep soft icing. It tasted of almonds and chocolate and spirits. We played a game. We made the cockroaches drunk by hawing on them and when we had lured them out of the crevices and stumbled up along the window-pane we made them doubly drunk so that they fell again and again. We were drunk ourselves. He was better at it than me. He could breathe out for a longer period. He said, 'They think it's summer.' But it was not. It was snowing on the mountains. Soon it would be snowing on the plains.

Dear Auro,

When I had fever he moved the commode in, crushed aspirins in water. He listened to my nightmare. People's tongues were in my mouth – outsize and nauseous – all kinds of tongues threatening to choke me. He said a nightmare was a female monster. He said how unfair that all monster things should be female. He stopped the clock in case the ticking irritated. Gave me honey from a spoon. Like a mother. He opened a window and guess – he trained the bough of a winter jasmine in. It did not blossom. As well as being a nurse, a doctor, a composer, a scientist, an inventor and a musician, he had been a tightrope walker. He said in a narrow street women sat making pillow lace and watched their men tightrope. In that narrow street I longed to be. I said, 'Herod, when will the piano-tuner come?' 'Soon,' he said, 'soon.' But the snow beat him to it.

Dear Auro,

The snow was a distraction at first, tossing and turning in the air, coating the tops of the pines but not the undersides, whitening the flat field that led to the sanatorium, making little difference to the mountains because the mountains always had it. Then one day the tops of the wooden posts were covered and I thought it was like a paw on each post and I began to think of it as a beast whose paws would go over everything. At night it was one level, but by morning it was another matter. He had got supplies in, smoked meat, smoked herring, flour, cheeses, wheat germ for vitamins, oranges, and a sack of very excellent potatoes. We were safe and so was the cow. The cow with her coarse brown coat the colour and texture of the shed she lived in. The cow with a yield of disgustingly rich milk. Man, woman and cow. We were safe within our prisons. In the cow-house a stench of manure and sweating hay, in the house a smell of fire and hen-dirt. The hens were brought in at night in their coop.

Concretions of snow built into cliffs and only two – narrow as margin – paths to hold on to. One to the cow-house, one to his music chamber. In the morning he milked the cow and I forked hay from the upper storey down to the manger where the cow, dazed, stupefied, but obedient, yielded milk. 'Are there rats?' I said. 'Bound to be,' he said. He went on ahead with the milk while I finished forking the hay. Something made me jump down, open the door and usher the cow out. Even the path was covered with a fresh fall of snow since the time I went in. The cow tossed her head, let out one of her dreary moans, and shat contentedly over the new snow. On its whiteness a treacle-coloured pat spread scutterishly over a big area. It made a crazy shape and the liquid trickling out defiled still more snow. And how I welcomed it: slime on the unlimited whiteness. A song. My first little rebellion. 'What the hell do you think you're doing?' He was standing in the kitchen doorway studying me, with his pre-war binoculars. I smiled to myself and turned my back so that he could not see my face. I led the cow back. I thought since I have come here a lot of things have broken out inside me: dissonance, cunning, madness and hate. The niceness can never be assembled again. I remained outdoors shovelling.

Dear Auro,

The falling snow was like ash. Ash that has risen from a bonfire, and is on the descent again. I felt happy, relishing my solitude. I opened my mouth and let the snow fall on my tongue. It tasted not of ashes. It tasted of pure cold. And I thought 'On certain days you are happy regardless of your predicament.'

Dear Auro,

We were by the fire, like stones, two stones, one waiting to burst. I said, 'I will tell you a story.' I began: 'There were birds on an island and they had been there for thousands of years and when the war broke out the island was needed but the birds got in the way of the landing planes. So they had to be got rid of. Many methods were tried, poison, gas, fumigating, bird-catching; none worked, until one day a man came with a needle and in the spring when the nests were full he pierced the eggs and over-night the birds flew away, they did not even wait for their young to be born because they knew that the snakes had come. They flew from the snakes they had never known . . .' And I looked and I saw that he liked that story very much, and I said, 'People will get up to anything, won't they?' And he said, 'Those birds have waited thousands of years for those snakes,' and I said, 'Poor birds,' and he said, 'Stupid birds.' It was like that.

Dear Auro,

He caught grasshoppers. He knew that to catch them you had to do it in the early morning before the sun sharpened their wits. He was very patient with them. He had such rapport with them. He was teaching them simple tricks and how to speak. He would devote hours to them. 'Oh Herod,' I thought, 'why does the slow poisoner in you win? You with so much of the saint, so much possible good, you the above average with one dead father, one dead mother and one faithless sister, what real or what invented wrongs has brought you to this?' But I never asked. Questions infuriated him. He thought questions were asked in order to over-throw him. (The day I mentioned his sister he was white with fury. I had found a photo of her with her name on it – Inge Clevering. She was his sister, a violinist, she was quite famous. He said she always had herself photographed front face because she lacked profile, she was as vain as that.)

Dear Auro,

He said, 'Many women project their family into their

later life and for some it is the only involvement they can have.' He said possibly I was repeating the ties with my father. I said I never knew my father which is the truth.

Dear Auro,

The first time I made an attempt to escape was in rain. I had not got as far as the sanatorium when out of nowhere he appeared like a spirit. He said, 'You were about to betray me.' His voice dreadfully calm, dreadfully normal. I said, 'One of the day-old chicks has got lost.' 'Ah,' he said, 'day-old love dies rapidly.' I pretended not to understand and I searched in the lower foliage for a tiny chicken. He said, 'You think of nothing else but escape, you dream about it, in your sleep you talk about it, you plot, you connive, but dear girl you wouldn't get far . . . to whom are you going, to what, you have no one to go to, you have severed all ties; a mad race up the drive might get rid of your fat or your bile but not your problem Willa, not your problem, think of you, the little virgin picking away at her clitoris . . .' I did not want to hear, I did not want to know about myself, I turned round towards home. It was useless. You have to be ready to go when you go, you have to be ready to swim when you swim, it is the same with hate, it is the same with all things. I turned round and went back. He followed me. Our voices answered each other under the suffocating trees and I thought and I knew, 'It has to go on . . .' The rain had stopped. It clung to the branches. The branches dissolved in wet gleams and so did I. So did reason. Some lunacy took charge of me and I asked to be forgiven. Forgiven for something I wanted to do!

Next day he staged a trial. I was given plenty of warning. He put a black eye-shade on me. It was made of fabric and fitted very well across the bridge of the nose. He had been given it on a polar flight. There were elastic ribbons for adjusting the tautness. He said I must be comfortable. He brought me to another chalet. He locked the door. The trial dealt mainly with my deceit. And after I had admitted to being guilty he said, 'Let's look at a few old photos, shall we,' and he reminded me of things confessed to him in the very beginning, in our halcyon days – words, images, bits of stories: crochet needles, cists, picked primroses wilting on a heath, cake-crumbs, the war, slippery elm for a woman, blood soaking through nine double layers of newspaper, the man who had wronged the woman sitting me on his knee and feeding me soft boiled egg from a spoon, the kitchen table the centre of so many crimes, the doctor sitting there with my mother, his hand tinkering in the unknown, later an operation on the same table without anaesthetic and gallons of Jeyes fluid . . .

When he took off the eye-shade I could see that we were in a ruin. Three walls were left standing but the fourth was only noticeable by the trench for its foundations. (Bolting the door had been a question of tactics.) The floor, mosaicked by green bird-droppings, led to the trench and was on a level with the field. You could smell the grass and I wondered why I hadn't smelt it during the trial or heard the airy distant sound of cow-bells. He pointed to the field and presumably to the world beyond it and he said, 'You are free to go now, nobody will drag you back,' but I did not move. I stood there, numb, rooted, will-less. I thought to surrender means utter peace. You see I was not quite dead in myself because I did have that small thought. He said there was certainly one thing he was grateful to me for – the way I kept him on his toes, the way he had to keep inveigling me with one little scheme or another. He linked me back to the house. 'One more walk of comrades,' he said.

Dear Auro,

How far we had gone on that mad road that started off so blithely – the sleighs, the kohlrabi, the humble kitchen garden flowers around which he had bandaged wet rag in the hope that they stay fresh and moist for ever.

Dear Auro,

He gave back my presents. Put them in my bedroom with a note saying, 'Second-rate presents are for others perhaps, but not for me.' And I thought, 'What do I do with a rustless wheelbarrow,' and I laughed, despite myself.

Dear Auro,

And oh, I have to say it, somewhere somewhere Herod loved me. A sunken love, a bitter love, but true. Because when I made my next attempt to leave he begged me to give him a little time, a little pity, to wait at least until Easter, because a man – even an intelligent man – gives in to sentiment at a time like that. He said he liked the idea of resurrection. He said every man deserved a second chance. Every woman too. I agreed to wait. He taught me to say 'Happy Easter' in German. It was a lovely night. I had broken it to him out of doors, thought it might be better. A lovely night with a sky swept bare of all but a moon. You could feel the spring. He said to wait at least until I saw the catkins. He said the catkins would be a sight to see. The white catkins swinging on the trees would become my people.

Dear Auro,

On the window-sill a square-necked bottle of mauve medicine. Like an unfinished medicine bottle on any kitchen window, its label defaced, the powder settled at the bottom, the liquid above only a pale reflection of the colour it would be if the bottle was shaken. He took it up and began to shake it. I had given him back his ulcer. And I prayed, I prayed it was the type of ulcer that burst and required immediate medical attention.

Dear Auro,

We went down the ladder stairway to his quarters four times in all. Once after the cliff walk, once after the rat got in, at Christmas and after my second aborted escape. Four times. I made lists of all things, all the people I'd ever met, the number of times I ate smoked salmon, the skies that had rainbows and the ones that had not, the joints of beef I had seen on pub counters. I made lists of conversations too. A woman said to me years before, 'It is thought that people dream only in black and white but I dream in colour.' A woman for whom I had made tea but had not allowed the water to boil. Grey tea with leaves floating on the surface. An unacceptable cup of tea for a woman who dreamed in colour. Venial crime but venial crimes add up.

Dear Auro,

When the rat got in he insisted that I accompany him while he shot it. The rat got into the store room to avail itself of the sack of very excellent potatoes. He made me hold the torch. He said he had every reason to believe that the rat was about to give litter. Had I heard of that phenomenon where rats born are all joined together by an enormous parent tail – heads, eyes, teeth, all varieties of fur congealed together in one enormous mass, and the tail, like a thong, thick and strong. That got me a little hysterical and I jumped on the table so that when the rat came from under it I was not sure which of us Herod shot at. He shouted as he shot at it. He shouted in German. Because I hadn't helped him by holding the light he said I would have to sweep it away, but I refused.

Dear Auro,

The piano-tuner turned out to be blind. His blindness came as a shock to me. I was sent by Herod to the avenue gate to escort him down. He was a middle-aged man, wearing two odd gloves. It was the same with the rest of his clothing. They had been bought with no regard for their size or their matching value. He asked what I looked like. He had not always been blind. He said that he'd been on a war mission that went horribly wrong. He gave me a little card. It had his name – Adolf Triska – printed on. He said Triska meant splinter. He said it was a very nice apartment. At least he had been told it was a very nice apartment and would I come some time.

Dear Auro,

I said to Herod, 'The piano-tuner was on a mission that went horribly wrong.' Herod said, 'He was on a mission in bed that went wrong in bed.' He said the blindness was due to syphilis. I asked how he knew. He said there were ways and means.

Dear Auro,

I sat by the fire holding pieces of paper on the end of tongs; watching them catch fire, blaze and curl up. Then as each piece of paper etherealized into ash I discarded it and got another and although I did not know it then, the plan had broken out inside my head. The plan was forming itself. Herod called from downstairs, 'Are you still up?' I thought, 'Do you want to know something Herod? You do not rule me any longer. If you want your power back, you will have to kill me.' 'I am not sleepy,' I said. 'Are you menstruating?' he said. He always claimed that menstruation did havoc to my emotions. I went to the door. The sawdust under the trestle was transformed into silver because of a light frost and I went out. I started to walk. It was an hour of night I suppose when he thought I would not go far. I did not think it either. I am frightened of darkness but it was a question of choosing between two evils. Of course I did not attempt the gallop that night but I took up the habit of walking and facing my dread of the forest and then when he least expected it – like each and every deserter – I left him high and dry.

Dear Auro,

But as Herod himself might say, 'Entries in the heart are not like entries in ledgers, they cannot be crossed out.' The more you try the more unsightly the inner page becomes, which is why I always say that memory is the bugger. You are for ever subject to it, subject to its gusts that can . . .

*

Auro knew it all now. He pieced together the various hints, he remembered little things about haircuts, or hawing on cockroaches. He knew why it was that she had to hold back and he pitied her as he had never pitied her in life. Yes, she had slept with him, she had taken a big chance and he admired that because in the circumstances it was quite brave. But he hadn't had her – not really – because he had not known her. If she were alive now he would give her a year, maybe longer, and between them they would get rid of Herod (poor mad bastard, impotent too) and make a woman out of her. He was ready to love as he had not been ready before. An unspent frustrating love, but a thing like that can rage and swell simply because it has no chance. It was racking him. And he had plenty of time, he had all the time in the world to keep going back over it. So had Patsy. So had Tom.

*

Tom had the most time. He used to go mad suddenly – anywhere, in the drill yard with the screw yelling, in the cauldron they called a kitchen (where out of perversity they put him to work), in the cell at night when he wasn't able to get to sleep. 'If only, if only,' he'd say, making one single alteration in that week's itinerary, bringing her back to life only to persecute himself still further. Patsy always knew when he'd had a recent bout because he used to be very quiet in himself, quiet and inert behind bars. She did her best to be cheerful, to bring the news, letters from home, plenty of fags, to hide her own hell – veins, shortage of money, not even a letter of commiseration from Ron, no way of knowing what he felt, what he knew, endless walks back to that street as if walks could undo a thing. There was loneliness everywhere. She never missed a visiting day, never. It wasn't that they forgave each other, it was that they were humbler as good people are when catastrophe tries to crush them. They knew that they were unimportant. They never considered blood tests when the baby came: because, as Patsy said, it was information they could very well live without.

More about Penguins and Pelicans

Penguinews, which appears every month, contains details of all the new books issued by Penguins as they are published. From time to time it is supplemented by *Penguins in Print*, which is our complete list of almost 5,000 titles.

A specimen copy of *Penguinews* will be sent to you free on request. Please write to Dept EP, Penguin Books Ltd, Harmondsworth, Middlesex, for your copy.

In the U.S.A.: For a complete list of books available from Penguins in the United States write to Dept CS, Penguin Books, 625 Madison Avenue, New York, New York 10022.

In Canada: For a complete list of books available from Penguins in Canada write to Penguin Books Canada Ltd, 2801 John Street, Markham, Ontario L3R 1B4.

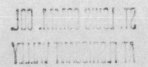

Edna O'Brien

The Country Girls

This famous first novel introduces two delightful
heroines, Kate and Baba, and a host of other Irish
characters in unpredictable situations.

Girl with Green Eyes

The comic and poignant sequel to *The Country Girls*
in which Caithleen Brady finds romance in Dublin –
classy romance with the second Mr Gentleman.

Girls in Their Married Bliss

Readers of the previous two novels will not be
surprised at the tragicomedy of the married lives of
Kate and Baba.

August is a Wicked Month

Ellen was alone in London, separated from her
husband. Bored and frustrated, she decided to go south
in search of sun and sex – but found it was not quite
as easy as that.

The Love Object

The heroine of each of these short stories swings in her
different way between euphoria and agonizing
disappointment.

A Pagan Place

In a stream of image, impression, expression, experience
and bitter fact of life, Edna O'Brien catalogues
the almost delicious agony of the poor Irish child.

Zee & Co

Edna O'Brien explores the sexual geometry of the
eternal triangle – and discovers some acute new
angles . . .